Scra  Mind:

Featuring Shirley and Willie Nelson and Many Others

Scrapbooks in My Mind:

Featuring Shirley and Willie Nelson and Many Others

Shirley Caddell Collie Nelson

Author's Note

I didn't originally intend to write a book. I set out to find out a few things about myself and about why the man I married decided to marry someone else. Strange what writing can do to an ordinary person. Try it sometime! I did. Hope you like it: Scrapbooks in My Mind.

-Shirley Nelson

To everybody involved in my life and career, I love you all.

Table of Contents

In the Beginning

In the beginning of the year 1931 people everywhere were singing, "Life is just a bowl of cherries." Little did anyone know by the end of the year, twenty thousand people would have committed suicide due to the failing economy of the country. And that was just a starter.

On a cold and snowy morning on March 16, 1931 at 1201 Calhoun, Chillicothe, Missouri at about 4:30 in the morning, a baby daughter was born to Alice Leona, a housewife, and Henry Simpson, a trucker. Dr. R. J. Brennan was assisted by the father's sister, Ms. Euliala "Layla" Rinehart, and by Mrs. Mata Davis, the baby's maternal grandmother.

When the baby arrived, her face was covered with a glossy "spider veil," which should have been dried so the child would have exceptional "gifts from God," so the old folks say.

Aunt Layla told the baby's father that the child had "a head like a horse." He almost fainted! All she had meant was that the baby's head was big and covered with a mane of golden hair. The doctor told the baby's father, "She's the most beautiful baby I've ever delivered," which he probably told all new fathers. They named her Shirley Angelina Simpson.

I would learn later that my aunts always had something negative to say.

The Little Martin

On December 22, 1941 at the Martin Company in Nazareth, Pennsylvania the "Little Martin" 00018 was born. The serial number stamped in the shop was 77925. The shop order was 576. She was fifteen inches long. Her back, sides and neck were mahogany. Her top was spruce and the overlay was rosewood.

She would be shipped to the Lyon Music Company in Kansas City, Missouri as soon as she was able to travel. Only 326 others of this model would be made for the world, and she would sell for sixty-seven dollars.

Little did anyone know that waiting in Missouri would be tender love and care from a young girl. This would be the first good guitar that girl would ever have. But it would be a few years.

You and My Old Guitar
Jimmie Rodgers (1933)

I could never be lonely,
I could never be blue,
I'll go through life if only
I have a guitar like you.
Why should I worry?
Why should I be sad?
We travel through life in a hurry,
Sharing the good and the bad.
Here we go—just you and me.
Oh how happy we will be.
We'll hitch our wagon to a star.
And I'll sing with you,
My old guitar

My Life with the Martin 00018 Guitar

The first time I held the Little Martin 00018 guitar I thought I'd died and gone to heaven! I was fourteen years old, fresh from the country and going to work at KMBC Radio in Kansas City, Missouri. It was 1945.

Guitar-Playing Chillicothe Girl Making Good on Roundup Radio Programs

When show people say they have been in show business 10, 12 or 20 years, Shirley Simpson, now only 17, can say she has been in the business for nearly all her life. Shirley began dancing when she was about 14 months old, so says her mother, Mrs. Henry Simpson.

It wasn't long after beginning to tap dance that little Shirley began dancing for friends and before service clubs here in Chillicothe. She went from there to guest appearances on radio stations and with professionals who played in this area. Last month Shirley signed a contract with radio station KMBC in Kansas City and now appears with another girl singer every week-day morning.

Shirley was born right here in Chillicothe on March 15, 1928. She can't remember when she began entertaining and has to rely on her mother's memory for actual dates, but one thing she is sure of and that is that she never had a lesson in learning any of the numerous dance steps she knows or on any of the number of musical instruments she plays.

By the time she was three years old, Shirley, or Sue as she is known in her program, could sing a number of songs. Her mother said that she picked up the words and melodies to the pieces from hearing them on the radio. "She would hear a song and then sing the melody and words as if she were reading them out of a book," her mother recalls.

Although there was no indication of music from her family, Shirley's

brother, Ronnie, 16, and sister, Mary Lou, 6, both show promise of following Shirley's footsteps. During the war, Shirley came into her own singing at bond rallies and

—Constitution-Tribune Photo.
SHIRLEY SIMPSON

on station KFEQ in St. Joseph as a guest artist. She had appeared earlier with a Chillicothe group in a national competition in St. Louis and shared the stage with well-known stars of radio and screen. Shirley was six at the time and the smallest performer there, according to press clippings of the event.

When she was 11 years old, Shirley wanted to learn to play the guitar. She didn't have the money,

(Continued on page 6.)

At this time I purchased the Martin from the girl whose place I was taking, for seventy-five dollars, which, to a country girl, was a huge amount of money. By now the guitar was four years old and the most wonderful thing to come into my life. My name was Sue of Millie and Sue.

KMBC BRUSH CREEK FOLLIES
Saturday Night, 8:30 P. M.
Millie & Sue
Night
plus
Dusty Rivers &
The Wagon Masters
Bill & Glenn
Anna Mae
Slaughter
Millie & Sue
Ray Holder Will Call the
Square Dance After the Show!
ADMISSION 61c
Air Conditioned Memorial Hall
Sponsored by 40 & 8 Voiture No. 762, American Legion,
K. C., K.

In the early years we traveled by car to jobs in many different states and worked with visiting stars of those days—such as the original Sons of the Pioneers. In fact, Hugh Farr, who was the bass singer for the Sons of the Pioneers, always kept the Little Martin in perfect tune because he loved to play it. Hugh would ask me, "Is she going out of tune? Well, better let me see." Then he would be able to hold and play it. And he would be a happy "Son of a Pioneer."

Every Saturday night we'd hear Hank Snow and George Jones. Then we'd go on to the Brush Creek Follies, which was an important barn dance show in the late forties.

Appearances by Roy Acuff, Gene Autry, Mother Maybelle and the Carter family with Chester Atkins of the famous guitar playing Atkins family, were not uncommon on the Brush Creek Follies.

After about five years I left KMBC to travel to Texas to play with Bob Wills, Johnnie Lee Wills and other Texas bands. I later settled in Corpus Christi to work on TV and with dance bands until I was offered work on the Ozark Jubilee with Red Foley in Springfield, Missouri. I stayed for two-and-a-half years.

[Me with Slim Wilson at the Ozark Jubilee]

While I was on the Ozark Jubilee, the Little Martin was played by Red Foley, Jimmy Wakely, Webb Pierce, Rex Allen, Porter Wagoner—everyone loved the tone and liked to rehearse with it. They gave me a new name, Shirley Caddell, and I used the Martin on all my recording sessions during those years. She was alive.

After working at the Ozark Jubilee, I was offered a job with the Philip Morris Country Music Show, out of Nashville. By that time I had a recording contract from ABC Paramount. I was twenty-two years old. We toured with many known artists of the fifties in all the states in the U.S.

Jimmy Dickens, Carl Smith, Goldie Hill, Biff Collie, Red Sovine, George Morgan—some of the best musicians out of Nashville—all played and loved the Little Martin.

We, the guitar and I, left the show in 1955 to marry Biff Collie and move to Hollywood to work on a show called "Country America," on ABC-TV. Then to add to our list, we were on *Town Hall Party* with Merle Travis, Joe and Roselea Maples, Tex Ritter, Bill Anderson, Hank Williams, Jr., Jeannie Sterling, who later became Bobby Bare's wife, and many of the legends of country. Merle especially recalled how he liked the way the Martin's strings set so low and what a wonderful neck and body she had.

Lady Guitar was what she was called and she was fourteen years old. I was on Columbia records and I was twenty-four years old. My name was Shirley Collie.

Then, after auditioning for "The Beverly Hillbillies" I got the part of the visiting aunt who comes down from the hills to sing, yodel and play guitar for them. I auditioned for Paul Henning, the producer, and he said the guitar and I belonged together. Bea Benadara was later to get it, because we, the guitar and I, ran away with Willie Nelson. I don't want you to think this was a spur of the moment thing, because it wasn't. I had been unhappy for a couple of years and was working too much. I'll tell you more about this later.

We left California for the hills of Tennessee by way of Canada, Texas, California again and finally Ridgetop, Tennessee. My name became Shirley Nelson.

Now, Willie completely fell in love with "Baby," as he named her, because she was so receptive to his every touch. He wrote beautiful songs with Baby playing the chords: "Healing Hands of

Time," "Pretty Paper," "It Looks Like a December Day," "Permanently Lonely," "I Never Cared for You." I wrote "Little Things" and "Once More with Feeling," which was recorded by Glen Campbell, and other songs, which I will list at the end of this book.

[A song Willie and I were working on]

"Lady Guitar," or "Baby," traveled with us and was played by Roger Miller, Merle Haggard, George Jones, all the people we were meeting on the road, such as Buck Owens and Ernie Ashworth, and at all Willie's sessions for Chet Atkins on RCA records. Will changed her strings to classical strings so she wouldn't hurt when she was played.

One funny story about Roger. We were in California for recording sessions and Roger asked to borrow her for a little while—

he wanted to write a song or two. Willie and he were good friends, so Willie let Roger take Baby. By midnight he hadn't returned and Willie and Jimmy Day went on a witch-hunt for Roger, starting out from the Knickerbocker Hotel in Hollywood. When he found him, Roger was in his car with Baby in his arms and he had written one of his most popular songs, "Dang Me." Later he was to write "K.C. Star" at our home, and he again wrote with Baby because she so inspired him. Anyway, with fire in his eyes Willie got his Baby back, unharmed.

If anyone was allowed to play her they couldn't use a pick. And if you drank you couldn't drink while playing her—no smoking and no cussin' were allowed, because she was a living creature and she was the tender age of twenty-one.

Years later in Austin, Texas, my grandson Anthony, who was seven years old, wanted to play the guitar and I said he could. When he got it out of the case my stepdaughter Susie screamed at me, "Get it away from him—he has a pick," and I laughed and thought back to a day when the sign read, "no picks allowed!"

The years 1963-1967 were Baby's happiest. She had a home, family, children and she was off the road—semi-retired after all the roadwork from 1941-1963. Now she was a songwriter's guitar at home and at recording sessions. Willie, the kids and I had come home to rest—but not for long.

[Willie at Bandera, Texas, Labor Day, 1968]

By October 1969, Baby was leaving again with me to go to Missouri, within ninety miles of where she came from. She was twenty-eight and beginning to mature. Her rich tone put me to sleep many nights when I lay awake. She helped me through bad times by being there to play the song-stories I wrote during the years 1971-1980. She's been there a lot and also on the brink of thirty-nine. I'm forty-nine.

Now she was being played from 1980 on through 1987 at social gathering, nursing homes, at midnight mass where her beautiful tone all alone in the church made you know she was alive; at prisons where I could tell the inmates she's never been pawned, no matter how hard times were. She's always been with me—and it's never too late to start over.

We were out and funning. From 1987-1989 I worked for the state of Missouri with the mentally disabled and the residents there loved to touch the strings when I played and lay their head on the sound box to hear her tone. Those who could not speak or see loved the Baby when she played, from 1990 to 1991.

There comes a time when your children or friends must leave you and after talking things over with my best friend Eddie Melton we decided due to health problems, mine, Baby must live on with a special someone. I've often wondered what would happen to her when I passed on. I had talked of Eddie taking care of her, but he felt she must continue. My reason is a simple one: She must be played and let others hear her. She's in fine shape, beautiful condition. All the handprints and love pats from everyone who've held her are still there. Everything is original, like she was when I first held her.

Lady Guitar is sixty-six years young. I'm seventy-six years old and my name is Shirley Caddell Collie Nelson. Thank you.

Back to the Beginning
1933-1937

TO PRESENT FLOOR SHOW

Mr. and Mrs. Carl Shirley of the Sugar Bowl will present little Shirley Ann Simpson, six-year-old daughter of Mr. and Mrs. Henry Simpson, in a floor show, including song and dance numbers, at the Sugar Bowl tonight at 9 o'clock. The little girl, who has recently appeared in broadcasts from St. Louis, Kansas City and St. Joseph, will broadcast again over the St. Joseph station KFEQ Saturday afternoon at 2:30. Her five-year-old brother and "manager" also will appear in the floor show. Songs and dancing will make up his act.

[My debut]

Daily Pick-Ups

Little Shirley Simpson, six years old, who has high aspirations about Hollywood and a dance career, is seemingly on the right track. She appeared on the Sid Kingdon Players program at the city hall Monday night and won instant favor. She will appear with them in several nearby towns this week.

Shirley has never had a teacher but she taps like a veteran and has some mighty good routines, especially for such a youngster. She gets all her ideas for new steps from the radio and few at her age can imitate so well.

The cute blue costume Shirley wore Monday night was made by her grandmother, Mrs. Ike Davis.

[My first review]

Mom and Dad and Grandma, I guess, must have told me that I was singing and dancing when I was two or three years old, but I really don't remember too much about it. I did have some pictures but I guess they fell along the way. Anyway, I was thinking about riding in a car. I guess you might say I was on the road then at two-to-three years old for money. Only fifty cents or a dollar but we could have a feast on that. Little towns around Chillicothe, fairs and that kind of stuff, oh yes, singing for the political parties—one year the Democrats and next Republicans. I never knew which I'd be—but that comes a little later.

TO PRESENT FLOOR SHOW

Mr. and Mrs. Carl Shirley of the Sugar Bowl will present little Shirley Ann Simpson, six-year-old daughter of Mr. and Mrs. Henry Simpson, in a floor show, including song and dance numbers, at the Sugar Bowl tonight at 9 o'clock. The little girl, who has recently appeared in broadcasts from St. Louis, Kansas City and St. Joseph, will broadcast again over the St. Joseph station KFEQ Saturday afternoon at 2:30. Her five-year-old brother and "manager" also will appear in the floor show. Songs and dancing will make up his act.

[Taking the stage]

[I'm the one with the big bow]

Dad always made Grandma sit in the middle of the back seat. My brother Ronnie was on one side and I was on the other. We went everywhere and, you know, he never had a map. We'd be on country roads and back roads, I remember. He'd stick his head out the window and ask Mom if she saw the Little Dipper or the North Star. I really never understood but I didn't have to. All I had to do was perform when we got there.

The reason why Dad had Grandma sit in the middle was she was a little bit heavy and he said, "You need to balance the wheels for us," and, "You won't break the shocks." She'd get so mad but she loved my dad, so she would do it.

I don't know what kind of car it was but Dad probably had put it together with spit and glue. What a man! He was the seventh of ten kids. Grandpa and Grandma split up and she took the girls and the boys went to work. I didn't know my Grandma Simpson. I only saw her twice in my life—once when Dad parked at the end of her country lane and my brother and I walked. Dad worked in a sawmill for Grandpa Simpson at six years old, went to school just one day, came home because he couldn't spell "egg." He also reminded me many times that the man who was sheriff then was in school and he couldn't spell "egg" either. He told me in later years that everything he ever wanted to do—Grandma and Mom were always against it. But he'd ask them and do it anyway! He was a railroad worker, laying ties for fifty cents a day, hauled coal for the State Correction School in Chillicothe. This was his big chance for money. He shoveled the coal off a big coal car by himself. I couldn't believe my eyes when I saw that he had done it. I don't believe he could either. He probably only weighed at the most all his life one-hundred thirty pounds and was five-foot-eleven, but he must have been uncommonly strong. He had a slender build. He had gentle eyes, quick temper, nice smile and a wonderful laugh. And he loved like crazy to tease people. Maybe that's where I get my sense of humor.

He finally was able to have his own trucks and haul livestock to market for everyone around Chillicothe and neighboring towns. I don't believe there was anyone he didn't know. He was the oldest self-employed trucker there. In fact the paper came to the house and did a story on him when he was seventy-nine. He was eighty years old when he stopped driving and only because he had a stroke. The doctor asked me on one of our visits, "What does he plan to do when he retires?" I laughed and told the doctor my dad didn't even know what retire meant. He didn't plan ever to retire. All he knew was to work. Dad laughed too. He passed away in 1988. I really miss him.

The best advice he ever gave me was, "If you don't succeed the first time that's all right, but if after a second try you'd better look things over—find out where you are—because butting you head into a brick wall is really stupid!" I guess that's the way Great Grandpa Simpson thought when he was in the Civil War. Three days before it was over he said, "I'm tired of this. It don't make sense. I'm going home to my family." And he did.

[Dad and Mom]

I'm not exactly sure where we came from—Illinois, I believe—but wherever it was I'm glad we came. I used to tease Dad about the pioneer spirit. Why didn't the folks go on west? Maybe because I love

Texas, but he'd tell me, "We did good to get this far, so accept it—you're a Missourian."

As for my brother, who sang and shimmy-danced and rolled his eyes and was my manager, Mom would put a big hat on him so he even looked smaller. He was about sixteen months younger than I was. We'd dance and sing and collect the contest money. Now this is BG, Before Guitar, so I know we had someone play the piano, but I'm not sure who it was. How did they get there? I gotta ask about that—the only lady I remember was from Waverly, Missouri. She had the most beautiful brown eyes and red hair I've ever seen and she could really play piano. Did I rehearse? I don't know. I don't think so. This is really funny—but we always won. We must have been doing something right!

A train hit Grandpa Davis's car in 1936 and killed him. Until that time my mom, dad, Ronnie and I lived with Grandpa and Grandma. He, my grandpa, didn't seem to like me all that well—at least it seemed that way to me—but he did like Ronnie. He'd hold him in his lap and rock him in the chair and talk to him a lot. Now maybe I might just be seeing this wrong, because for about a year during this time I was really sick.

Shortly before Grandpa died, I had a ruptured appendix, then peritonitis. I don't think Mom and Dad believed in operations or it could have been we didn't have any money, but anyway, Mom and Grandma saved me by wringing out hot turpentine towels and putting them on my stomach all night long. I recall that Dad called a deathwatch and all his sisters came and sat around me. Doctor Brennan came and made them get out. He said they were taking up my air and I couldn't breathe. I remember learning to walk again and being outside in a chair in the sun.

Grandma was always baking pies for Grandpa for supper, and Ronnie would bring me sugar pie dough with cinnamon on it, mainly because I wasn't supposed to have it. One of these times when I was out in the yard, a big black car drove up to the house and Mr. Norman, who was the undertaker, went up to the door. Grandma had flour sugar on her apron when she answered and I heard him say to her, "Where do you want us to take him?" I didn't understand that a train had hit Grandpa's car and killed him and he wouldn't be coming home anymore, and Grandpa was in that big black car outside, dead.

Sometimes I would ask Grandma where Grandpa was, and she'd take me outside at night and tell me, "Look in the sky. The brightest star shining is your Grandpa." I still look up to see the star. I haven't forgotten.

Grandpa and Grandma were from Ohio originally.

They came to Chillicothe from there. I think at one time Grandpa had money, but when the banks closed in the thirties his money went with them. He traded and bought livestock after that for people all around the country. He was short, stocky, and balding and wore little round glasses. Dad kept a check for a long time that had been given to him in 1936, which he never cashed. After Grandpa's death I remember Mom had a nervous breakdown and was in bed for several weeks. So Grandma, who was so strong, had all of us to take care of for a while. I hadn't started school yet and Ronnie and I were sort of in limbo about singing and dancing but something else was about to happen that would change me for the rest of my life. I was about to discover the guitar.

From where we had lived on Cherry Street, we seemed to move an awful lot after Grandpa's death. I'm not sure if it was because we couldn't pay the rent or just because we were moving people, I just really don't know. One story about moving I will never forget. We had moved into a home and we hadn't been there very long but I found a girl I could play with. This girl, Connie Chapman had a gorgeous house, her own bedroom, dolls, and toys, like something out of a storybook. I had gone to play with her one afternoon and when I came back to the house where we lived, I opened the door and the whole house was empty. Can you imagine me running from room to room, scared out of my wits? My family moved away and didn't take me with them. I was yelling and screaming for Grandma, who heard me and came out of the house just across the street. Was I ever glad to see her! I hugged her, promised always to be good and everything else I could think of. Grandma said, "I thought your Mother told you we were moving across the street." But she hadn't. Anyway, I felt safe with Grandma and I knew it wouldn't happen again. Then Mom and Dad got a chance to rent rooms for us at 1100 Locust Street from Mrs. Shriver. She was a tall white-haired lady with a wonderful face full of smiles. She could also be tough too.

[Grandma, Mom, Marcella (friend), and Betty Davis]

I don't know how many rooms she had, but there were lots of people around. The woman across the hall from us must have been sickly 'cause she stayed in bed all the time and worked crossword puzzles. Once in a while I would visit with her and she showed me how to do the puzzles. I believe we called her "Auntie" but I don't think that was her name. She really increased my vocabulary;

anyway, I also thought she had TB. I didn't know what that was but during the thirties, every time someone got sick they had TB.

Mrs. Shriver let me do chores for her, like clean the bathroom upstairs and clean the hallway and stairs. I don't recall how much she paid me—ten or fifteen cents, probably.

The house was four stories, counting the basement, where she lived and had her kitchen. Basement, rooms on the first floor, up a stairway to the second floor, up a stairway to the third floor, up a stairway to the attic, my favorite place. We had electrical storms then, and when it would storm I'd run up to the attic and put my face in the window. Pretty soon Grandma would come after me. She always knew where I was. She'd tell me, soon as it rains all the danger is over and it always was, but did I ever love to look at lightning and listen to the "Tater Man," which was thunder rolling across the sky. She also told me when I saw cows lying down in a field it meant rain but I don't know too much about that. It could only be they're tired and resting, but at this point, if Grandma said it, she was right!

Let me describe Grandma to you. She had red-gold hair that really never changed much all her life, and pretty, soft, blue-gray eyes. She was only four-eleven and maybe a little bit chunky. After she found out she had diabetes she lost quite a bit of weight. She loved to dress up but for everyday she always had to have a clean dress, her hair fixed and her apron on. Never wear a dirty apron was her motto. She also always wore some kind of jewelry, usually earrings. In later years whenever I was away from her I never forgot to bring her some jewelry, especially earrings, and I never forgot Grandma. She loved detective books, the kind with the worst pictures I've ever seen.

[Me with Mom and Grandma]

The only other thing was that she'd smoke cigarettes. She'd never inhale, but she'd smoke. She always had a puff of smoke around her head. Believe it or not it looked like a halo! She had the most beautiful skin—smooth and not wrinkled at all. Even when she died and I looked down at her face in the hospital her skin was so smooth I had to touch it. All I saw was one single tear on her cheek. If anyone went to heaven, she did. She lived to be over ninety, but as long as I live she lives too!

I remember a lot about the house on Locust Street. It was a big three-story house with a basement and it's still there today. It had apartments and rooms. There, I remember learning to cook for everyone at the ripe old age of eight. I cooked, believe it or not, pork steak, fried potatoes with onions, sliced tomatoes and radishes from the garden, and I'm sure we had pie or cake. These were the years of plenty and my folks were now taking care of the roomers and we were doing all right. Mrs. Shriver was getting ready to go back to Kansas and she was gathering up all her things and we were going to move out of the two rooms we had. But Grandma would still keep her bedroom upstairs and I'd still stay with her at night.

On one occasion, Mrs. Shriver and I went to the attic to see what treasures she had up there. She was looking around and up on the shelf inside a huge closet was a small brown guitar. I asked her to let me see it and she told me it wasn't any good, just a piece of junk.

Well, that piece of junk became something to me.

I asked her if I could have it and she said no, but you can work for it. It would probably sell for around seventy-five cents if the junk man came by and I told her I would do it. I figured I'd already made twenty-five cents just following her around.

It seemed like I worked forever, but actually, only two days later she said, "It's yours. But how are you going to play it without strings?" Strings hadn't occurred to me. I guess they must have been fifty cents a package. So I was back in bondage again. She probably was smiling at me. I was a very determined person or maybe just a pest. Later I got the fifty cents and then I tried to figure out what to do next. I knew Mr. Reynolds who ran the music store. So I asked if I could go uptown and Mom told me yes, if I'd hurry back. It was only about three or four blocks and no one in those days thought anything about kids walking the street. Mr. Reynolds took my money, put some strings on it and tuned it, and back home I went.

In the books where I read music, words to sing, up above the words there was a picture of something that looked like a guitar neck and it had dots of where to put your fingers so I looked at these. To this day I still do the wrong fingering on some chords, but it doesn't seem to bother my playing. The strings were so high off the neck that my fingers were really sore by the time I'd tried to play a few chords. Then I noticed something was wrong. The guitar didn't sound right so, I asked Mom to take me back to Mr. Reynolds. Sure enough it was out of tune. Mom asked Mr. Reynolds if I was wasting anybody's time and he told her he didn't think so. I told him what I was doing with the music books and then he took a guitar book off the shelf and showed me the right way it could be done. He didn't give me the book, but on a sheet of paper he drew a picture of several chords. I believe it was D-A-G. He told me to come back when I needed him and he'd be glad to tune it. But he told Mom that I'd be tuning that old guitar myself before very long. That it was natural for me to hear it. If I were really interested I'd do it. If not, I'd put it away.

Believe me, I was an interested seven-year-old. I played and played at it when I wasn't doing my chores after school, before school—anytime I could—but I was having a great deal of trouble changing chords and making chords. I'm not going to tell you I was an overnight success at this. I wasn't. A year or more it's a wonder my folks didn't smack me but they didn't. Then I decided I had to take drastic measures. I had to have another guitar. Dad left early of a morning to haul coal and I was usually up anyway. So I asked him if I could have a new guitar or a better one, I believe I said. He told me if I could completely sing and play a song without stopping when he got home he would get one for me. I worked like a demon and when he came in and we had eaten supper, I propped myself up in front of him and played "Beautiful Brown Eyes." I sang it all the way through, all the verses too.

The first line of that song is, "Willie I love you my darling." Isn't that something that at the age of eight or nine I was singing about someone named Willie? I would marry a Willie twenty years later with beautiful brown eyes. Willie Nelson.

Need I say Dad was shocked not by the song but by my playing. He looked at me, he looked at Mom and Grandma who were both shocked and then he told me that we couldn't buy anything yet. No money. I laid the little brown guitar down, I hugged his neck and there were tears in his eyes. I went down the stairs and to the back steps and sat there and cried.

About a year later, I did get a guitar, a white one. It cost eleven dollars and it was beautiful. I shined it every day. Mom picked chickens and Dad did some extra work for Mrs. Shriver before she moved and I had, I don't know, what kind it was, a wonderful new guitar. I was playing and changing chords and Ronnie and I were singing for war bonds and on street corners on Saturday in front of Slater's Market and anywhere else they'd have us and we were back in business. I was carrying my guitar in a pillow case sack my Grandma made me. I was "hot stuff." Years later I would be carrying the Little Martin in a beautiful lined case but at this time there wasn't anyone more proud of anything than me. I never did keep any money I ever made. It went to the family.

Remember I told you about political affairs. We always did them and Grandma would be there. There would be those long, long speeches, then we'd sing, and then more speeches. This was probably a contract deal, and I think Mom made it. In fact, maybe she was political-minded. She always drove the car and picked up people to vote.

After one election night, it was late, 'cause Ronnie and I were asleep, and Dad woke us up. He said he wanted us to see something and do you know we went back in Grandma's room and, wonder of wonders, we had a baby sister. Naturally my comment was, "Who's that?" He told us she belonged with us. I never really had a relationship with Ronnie. He would come sing with me but otherwise, he didn't seem to like me. Maybe it was because I made more money than he did. I never really got to know him. Now all I could think about was one more person in two rooms, but she was little and I loved her.

Me and Mary Lou

Mary Lou, May 6, 1941. She was cute. I liked to wheel her uptown on Saturdays. I'd get her a two for a nickel ice cream cone and she'd spit it all over me. All I really wanted to know was where she had come from and why didn't someone tell me about these things, but you didn't ask questions like that when you were my age. What were the facts of life? I had a guitar, and two girls I went to school with had doctors for dads. They'd say come over and we'll look at doctor books but I couldn't see where that would be any fun at all. I'd rather look where you put your fingers on the guitar.

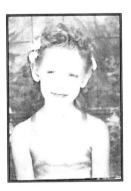

[Me at six]

[Mary Lou at six]

[Me and Mary Lou]

[Mary Lou, Me, and Willie]

We used to have well-known entertainers that came to the theaters in Chillicothe for shows. During one of these times Mom loaded me and my guitar in the car and had me play for Foy Willing of the Riders of the Purple Sage. I had seen him in the movies and I was really impressed. He told me I should stop playing with a thumb pick and play with a straight pick, so that's what I did. He also told Mom I really showed a lot of promise. I never could figure out if she was trying to convince herself I was pretty good or someone else. Anyway she managed my first interview with a star. No one ever told me I did well. That would have been boastful. Later Grandma told me she liked to hear me play and sing and Mom and Dad would fight over who taught me to yodel. I'd just look at them both and wonder if they did teach me, why didn't they do it. But if they liked to fuss, and they did, and each one wanted to say they taught me, so be it. I had a lot of thoughts when I was a kid. Mainly I believe I'm a dreamer. The only person I really talked to in the beginning was Dad. Later on, because she was always with me, I always talked to Grandma.

I figure you are wondering why I haven't talked much about my mother. It's very difficult. Maybe you'll understand if I tell you what I said to her after I came back home after being away for twenty-five years. I just said, "Mom if you knew me you might like me." She didn't answer me. I believe in my heart she is a good person but I just don't know what she wanted to do all her life. If I did I'd have moved heaven and earth to help her do it. She died in 1996 and she never did tell me what she'd like to have done.

Me and Millie: Millie and Sue

1945. I had heard about an opening for a girl singer on KMBC in Kansas City. I convinced my folks that maybe we should call and see what it was all about. We, my folks and I, didn't use the telephone very much and especially not for long distance, but Dad said O.K. Mom called and they wanted me to come audition with Millie of Millie and Sue. Seems Sue was leaving to be with her family and they needed a replacement for her. Had I known at that time they were auditioning several more girls I might not have gone. I probably would have thought I wasn't good enough. Anyway, Dad had some people that he hauled livestock for who needed to go to Kansas City and Dad asked if I might ride along and if they would take me to the Pickwick Hotel where the radio station was located.

Picture this with me if you can—I'm fourteen years old, I think Kansas City is the biggest place with the tallest buildings I've ever seen, I remember I had twenty-five cents for a sandwich if that became necessary, I'm going to have to ride in an elevator, and I'm scared. So I get on the elevator. It only goes to the tenth floor, KMBC is on the eleventh, I have to go up this stairway, which was spooky to me at that time and I'm alone.

The receptionist asked my name, what I wanted and I told her. Then she called back into some office and the girl that came to meet me was Millie, a.k.a. Lawana Wells. Well, she had a big smile on her face and the first thing she said to me was, "You're so young." I liked the smile and I knew I was too young, so I smiled, too! Later she told me she knew as soon as I smiled I was the girl she wanted.

We went back into this big studio and she said," Did you bring a guitar?" I said I didn't, so she handed me the Little Martin that later I would buy from Millie's sister, Sue. I began to play and sing some songs I knew. Then she started playing the mandolin and it really was good! I was laughing and enjoying myself, not realizing on the other side of a studio glass that was dark all the bigwigs were watching me. Mr. Roger Cupp, the program director, Fran Allison, music director, news announcers and some of the entertainers that appeared on the Dinner Bell Roundup and the Brush Creek Follies, which I listened to every day and on Saturday nights. I only found this out later.

Millie seemed to like me really well. We could sing well together and our voices blended. She told me I should go on back to Chillicothe and when everyone decided who was the one she would call and let me know. She rode downstairs with me and waited until the people I had ridden with came for me. I really had no idea the job was mine and a week later she called and said, "Come on down. You're on the air with me." I started screaming and Dad had to shake me to make me stop.

I hadn't thought of all the many things we had to do. The radio station would get Grandma Davis and me a utility apartment—that meant with a little kitchen—and I had to have costumes and boots and I had to sign a contract. Actually I didn't sign. My mom did because I wasn't sixteen yet. And Millie kind of paved the way for me, because her sister Sue and I were about the same size. I could buy her stage clothes and, bless her heart, I could buy the wonderful Martin guitar I had played, for only seventy-five dollars, if I had that much—which I didn't—but Millie introduced me to the Credit Union at the radio station. The accountant gave me the money to pay Sue and he would deduct five dollars from my salary every week until it was paid. I could have the Little Martin and they would deduct it from my pay.

[Millie and me at Dinner Bell Roundup KMBC with Rex Allen]

So Grandma Davis and I moved to Kansas City to a little apartment across the street from Millie and Archie, her husband, I had a 5:30 A.M. program every morning except Sunday, the Dinner bell Roundup at 12:00 noon, and the Brush Creek Follies on Saturday night at 8:00 P.M. Good Lord, I got to take care of Grandma and myself and Good Lord almighty I was making twenty-eight dollars a week and five dollars for every personal appearance on the road. I was practically a millionaire!

[Among the well-known groups that appeared on the original Brush
Creek Follies and Dinner Bell Roundup were
the Oklahoma Wranglers]

My first days at the radio station were something else. Grandma
would get up at 4:30 A.M., fix me bacon, eggs, toast, and jelly before I
went to sing for fifteen minutes on the air at 5:30. Millie would come
over about twenty minutes later, because we walked to work, take me
by a cafe (we pronounced it calf-aye), we'd eat pancakes, so
consequently a few months later I resembled a five-foot two
redheaded tank. Then one winter morning a little while later it was
snowing. I slipped off the curb. I had on a Teddy Bear wool coat. It
didn't hurt. I just rolled like a barrel into the street laughing. I looked

up at Millie, who was extremely slim and I heard myself say, "What does the word diet mean?" So she told me, plus any word I didn't understand she would tell me what it meant. Like one day in the elevator with Hoby Schelp and his friends Harold Willis, brother to the Oklahoma Wrangler Willis's, said, "I think I'll go back to my old job." Someone said, "What was that?" and he said, "Being a pimp."

When we got downstairs I asked Millie what a pimp was. She looked at me with that smile that she had and proceeded to tell me. I think my reaction was, "Oh, my, I didn't know anybody did that. I'd better tell Grandma."

Now back to the diet—no more potatoes, no gravy, no bread, and oh, how I loved bread—and a lot of other things like two breakfasts every morning. I think maybe I made Grandma feel bad, but she kept on making homemade cinnamon rolls and hot apple dumplings so I could stand the pain. And I began to lose some pounds and suddenly I sort of thought I might be pretty and the first time we made our public appearance together I thought I looked great. Someone in the audience whistled. Of course it could have been for Millie. She was a doll!

Let me tell you a little about being on the road in the late forties. There were no motels or hotels really fit to stay in, only cafes along the road, and not many of those. Everyone traveled by car, no silver eagles, in the forties and as many people in the car as possible. I met so many musicians and entertainers on the road later that were lying down in the back seat trying to sleep, so the only way I could recognize them was to have them bend their heads over. Funny?

But in the car when I rode, I was fortunate—Millie and me—Colorado Pete and Jed Starkey, who did comedy on the shows, who in real life was about as far away from comedy as possible. I guess I didn't realize that a woman on the road or in the entertainment business at that time wasn't very well looked upon. In other words, you didn't have a very good reputation being an entertainer. But I probably didn't know what "reputation" meant so I was happy as a lark. They didn't even call our music "Country." They called us "Hillbillies."

[1990. Seems like I'm back here again in Hillbilly land, just a little over two hundred miles from where I began.]

The Little Martin is still with me, maybe scarred up a bit but not enough to hurt her. She'd be hurt if she wasn't here with me. She's still helping to write songs and put together the pieces of my life.]

My First Steady Job

In the beginning or after the beginning, I really didn't want to be an entertainer. I was a dreamer and being a dreamer led to lots of ideas and things I wanted to be. My idol was my eighth grade English teacher, Mrs. Elliott. She'd let me be teacher's pet and she and I really talked about many different things. I told her that I wanted to teach and she suggested that I teach country school after graduation. At that time if you went to summer school, then you could start teaching all grades up to the sixth.

I told my dad and mom and they just could not find a way to meet expenses for me in a situation like that. I talked to Grandma too. She explained to me that Dad had it hard enough with all of us, his trucks, the men he had to have to help him and she also told me he had a chance to buy the big house we lived in for six hundred dollars. But he felt he shouldn't go into debt any more. I know that house sold for a lot of money several years ago, but then six hundred dollars was a huge amount of money. Anyway, no teaching job.

So I continued on dreaming and wondering what in the world was going to happen to me. Was I just going to graduate and fade away into the sunset? Can you imagine a thirteen-year-old flop? That's where I thought I was until one phone call changed things for me, and that call came from Kansas City, Missouri. And Millie Wells.

Everything that happened after the phone call that I had gotten the job in Kansas City seems kind of funny. I don't remember getting to the city, but we did. I don't remember packing, at least not like I do now, but we did. Seems like Grandma took her skillets along and probably a coffee pot, she had to have her coffee. Me, I probably didn't take much of anything, a few clothes, some music books, because I knew I was going to get the Little Martin. I didn't even take my beloved white guitar. I believe Ronnie took it for himself.

I think Mom took us to the city, but she didn't stay, only just signed a contract for five years. I was fourteen years old and I'd be nineteen when the contract was over.

Mr. Cupp the program director was very kind to me that day. He asked me if I understood what Mom was doing and I said I did. She was signing me away to a radio station for five long years, but I was happy about it. The next day my first show would be the "Dinner Bell Roundup" at noon. Millie and I rehearsed something that afternoon, but I can't remember what it was. It was probably "Remember Me" or "Echo from the Hills." We did sing those well together.

The next day at noon I know my teeth chattered. I was scared! All the people I'd listened to were suddenly listening to me. You know, the station decided not to say the other Sue was leaving, so I just stepped in and took her place and my name became Sue. I'm wondering now if I would have said something about that if I'd been older than fourteen, but maybe not. All I knew was—and I don't mean this to be boastful—but everyone said we, Millie and Me, sounded better than ever before, and I had the Little Martin at last for my own, thanks to the credit union at KMBC.

I know and I knew then that you're not supposed to place so much value on material things but the Little Martin was not just a guitar; it was my friend, just like a person. Our theme song for our morning show at 5:30 A.M. was "Echo from the Hills." The first line is "I'm a long way from home," and I was from Chillicothe. Grandma and I lived just down the street from the station in Kansas City, and everything was wonderful. Millie and I rehearsed quite a bit. She sang harmony, played the mandolin, and she was great. Millie was from Cross Timbers, Missouri, down by Springfield. I asked her how did a place get a name like that? She told me, "Two logs fell across the road and that's what they named it."

Millie always looked nice. She was about five-four or five-five and very slim, with dark hair and pretty brown eyes. I liked brown eyes. They always seem so sincere. Blue eyes like mine that turn colors always seem to flit around looking at everything and in those days I was surely doing that.

Millie, I'm sure, had her hands full with me, though I'd always been able to take criticism, and discipline. I really felt grown-up at least in my mind. Mr. Cupp had already had a talk with her and told her she would have to look out for me on the road with the guys, whatever that meant. The first few days I was in and out of love with somebody every few minutes. What a difficult job she had on her hands, and she just flat out told him she could handle it, and she did.

I was so naive. When she wasn't around the jokes and stuff they, mostly Ray Hudgens of the Rhythm Riders, played on me were really funny. One day everyone was sitting around in the lounge waiting until airtime at noon and Ray said to me, "Shirley go back to the music room where we got our sheet music and words and ask the director if you can have the words to "I'd like to see my old gal flow again." Off I went as fast as I could and announced to the whole world what Ray wanted. Everyone started laughing and I couldn't figure out why.

The guy, John Gilbert, the head of the music department, was kind of strange anyway. For lunch he always had a peanut butter, onion and mayonnaise or salad dressing sandwich as I called it. He told me to go back and tell Ray he can't help him out. When I got back to the lounge everyone there was laughing and Millie walked in and looked at me. She asked me, "What did they do to you now?" I told her. I know I still didn't get the joke. What Ray asked me to do for him and she took Ray into another studio and gave him a piece of her mind. All I could figure out was that must have been some piece of music to make everyone laugh so much. It was quite a funny welcome to the real world.

In those days of radio there were no taped programs. You always did your shows live whether you'd been on the road the night before or not. So I'm not going to say everything was roses. It was difficult but I was used to getting up early anyway, so the early morning didn't hurt me much. All that driving in the car with three other people was the hard part. Jed Starkey, our comedian always took the back seat and he'd lie down and sleep off and on. Millie was into cross-stitch dishtowels and so Colorado Pete, whose real name was George Martin, and I more or less tried to get along. I don't know why, but at first we seemed to fuss a lot. I think he fussed and I listened. Later on I got to where I'd talk back at him, but much later. But then I didn't want to lose my job and have to go back to Chillicothe. Maybe he just resented women on the road. I really don't know what it was. Jed always wanted to listen to the news. I wanted to listen to music and everyone else just wanted peace.

As I told you there weren't any fancy motels and restaurants like now and later on when we got out of Kansas, I mean way out, you could drive for miles and only see dust. We worked free shows for the people who sponsored by John Deere or Massy-Ferguson farm implement companies. We'd get into town, go to the store and check in, find out where the show was and often just wait around. We always had big crowds. Mostly folks listened to us on our radio shows and they felt they knew us. Colorado Pete, (why Colorado I'll never know), would open the show. Then Millie and I would go on, then Jed with comedy, and finally all of us together would do a closing song.

Let me tell you about Jed. To me he looked old. I don't think he was but he acted that way. On stage he was funny but offstage, watch out! When we'd go eat, none of us would sit with him. He'd order something, then he'd ask the waitress if she expected him to "eat this slop," or else he'd say this wasn't what he ordered. Most times he wouldn't have to pay. That's why he did that, I think. He was so tight, but funny. I really didn't understand but I was warned not to sit where he did. Anyway I was always with Millie. I'll never understand this either.

All Millie ever ate was poached eggs or cream of wheat, with dry toast. YUCK! But she said her stomach always bothered her. Me, I didn't know what stomach problems were. All I wanted to do was eat. But you know I always felt maybe my manners weren't good enough. Or maybe I was just shy about eating around other people. I'd always eat something that I didn't have to chew too much, or something I didn't have to cut too much. I was afraid if I had to cut something it might go into my lap. But of course it never did.

One funny incident about Jed's eating. We stopped in a little cafe way out in Kansas and I mean this place was little. Only one girl was taking care of the whole thing. Jed of course sat at the counter and we—Millie, Pete and I—sat over at a table. You could see back into the kitchen, where there was only a little, two-burner tabletop stove. Jed ordered a cup of coffee, drank about half of it and asked the girl if she could heat it up a little. She took his cup, went back in the kitchen, poured it into a small pan, put it on the stove and then brought it back to him. If you understand what Jed looked like you can understand when I make this next statement. He was about five-foot-three or four, spindly, dark-looking man with a nondescript face. Got the picture? He jumped off that stool and in my mind I saw Rumpelstiltskin from Grimm's Fairy Tales jumping up and down in front of the waitress. It was really funny. I didn't laugh then but I do now. Anyway that sort of tells you what kind of cafes we had to deal with and about Jed's encounters.

Another time, he ordered oyster stew. No one in his right mind would order oyster stew out like that, but he did. After he had eaten some of it, he pushed the bowl back, barked something at the waitress and she called the manager, then he just walked out. I couldn't wait to get to the car to find out what happened. This is the story he told us. He ordered oyster stew, when he looked down in the bowl, there was these sickly, puny, oysters swimming around in milk not hot enough to kill them. He crumbled his crackers in the bowl and before he could take a bite, the oysters came up and ate his crackers. Only a comedian could think of something like that. I just wonder what the manager of that cafe thought. No wonder entertainers got a bad name.

Another time—and this is not a Jed story but a true one—some musicians were traveling and of course everyone got hungry, but there was no money and no cafes. Anyway, they happened to pass a country church and there was a reunion going on and an all-day dinner on the ground. They pulled over, looked at the situation and decided everything, mainly the food, looked mighty good.

So they just got out of the car, went right up to the tables and began to eat. No one said anything about them eating. The only questions were, "Which side of the family do you belong to?" I suppose they had some good answers, 'cause they got filled up and they just left. I wonder if that could have been Hank Williams's band. Guess I'll never know but we all did crazy things like that.

On several occasions movie stars came to our radio station, including Gene Autry, Sunset Carson, Rex Allen and all the biggies of those days. Either they would guest on the daytime shows or Brush Creek Follies. Gene Autry, who I'd watched all my life in the movies, brought his radio show, "Melody Ranch," for a whole week to KMBC. Funny, I thought that naturally he'd know me because I'd watched him all my life in the movies. But he didn't, and I'm sorry to say he wasn't very friendly to me.

The guys I did meet were the "Sons of the Pioneers." What a group! Bob Nolan, Tim Spencer, Carl Farr, minus Roy Rogers, of course. He had gone on to become a cowboy star right up there with Gene Autry.

I guess I believed I was really somebody, getting to be around all these famous people. The Little Martin and I were as happy as could be. She, the Little Martin, was all of five years old and of course I was fifteen by now so we were really buddies. I never left her at home, or out of the case in the cold or warm air. She always had new strings and the tone she made gave you have the chills. It was so pretty and melodious.

If you've ever been around or had a chance to read about guitars, you know the mellow with age and I suppose both of us, the guitar and I, were beginning to mellow a little bit. Of course I had a long way to go but I didn't mind. I seem to have plenty of time.

I remember Roy Acuff, before he became the host of the Grand Ole Opry, coming to the Brush Creek Follies in 1946. He brought his complete show and my folks came down from Chillicothe to see him. It was really unusual for Dad to come. Roy had a duo in his show called, Lulabell and Scotty. I always wished that I could have been Lulabell. He was about the nicest man I'd ever met. He said I was a very pretty girl, so young and sweet, and he gave me a kiss, then went out front to meet my folks. I was so thrilled that I could be walking with Roy Acuff, out in front of the theater and he would be willing to say hello to my family.

Dad and Mom were really impressed that he was so nice and friendly. The touring shows of those days were packed with dynamite talent and I would stand in the wings with my eyes and mouth wide open probably trying to look sophisticated about the whole thing. When I look back now I can see I was really star-struck by people. Shows in those days were different than now. They didn't need security or backstage passes. If you wanted to say hello to someone you just walked up and said hello.

Mother Maybelle Carter and the Carter Sisters, Helen, June and Anita and Chester Adkins came in one Saturday night to guest on the Brush Creek Follies and I fell in love with the music they played. The way Anita sang was so beautiful and pure.

June was so funny running all over the stage doing her little comedy bit. She played the Autoharp and when Mommie Maybelle played "Wildwood Flower," I decided I was going to give some of that music a try.

Millie and I stayed pretty much up on all the music of the 1940s, including "I Couldn't Believe It's True," an Eddie Arnold song, "Blue Eyes Cryin' In The Rain," "Blues Stay Away From Me," "Put My Little Shoes Away," a real tear jerker, some really great story songs.

I was talking to a friend of mine recently, Don Sullivan, from the radio days at KMBC. He asked me, "Do you realize how many songs you did or knew in those days." I guess I didn't. Millie always worked out the program sheet. We were a Broadcast Music International (BMI) station even way back then. I'll give you an idea on our morning show. What we did was about five or six songs. Millie always played a hoedown on the mandolin, to wake up the cows. I liked "8th of January" myself. So if you figure five to six songs a day, one or two for Dinner Bell Roundup that would be about 170 to 200 songs a month. We weren't supposed to repeat any songs for at least four to six weeks. So I was really building a catalog of songs for myself.

Later on, at the Ozark Jubilee, Red Foley would always single me out and tell me to "get the 'Little Martin' and come and sing me some old songs." His favorite was "Are You Lonesome For Me Annabelle." It must have had a very special meaning for him 'cause sometimes the tears would roll down his cheeks and he'd tell me to sing it again and I would.

I probably know more old, old songs and different versions of old folk songs than anyone else I know, and I don't mean to be bragging. I can always picture the words in my mind and there they are just like a printed page. I've never kept a diary or scrapbook. It's simply all in my mind as if it was written there. I really thank God for that. I don't have any other answer as to why I can see it so clearly.

The year at the radio station and being on the road showed this country girl one thing for sure. Everything is always changing. Nothing stays the same. That's the way of the world. For someone who was only fifteen, I had made a mighty important discovery about life.

The word for the day is change and everything for me was about to do just that.

Boys and Dating ... and my First Marriage

Up to this point in my life I'd never dated anyone, except one date I had to go to the movies, to see the Saturday afternoon cowboy show. I guess I was about ten years old. As we started off walking to the picture show F. R. Bailey looked at me and asked me if I had a dime. Of course I did! I wouldn't think of going to the pictures without my dime!

Dating didn't really mean all that much to me. I had my guitar and my singing jobs so what else did I want? Mom had me so scared of boys before I left home. I just knew if you ever let them kiss you you'd be in the family way. Whatever else they'd do I didn't want to hear about. I'm not going to say I didn't have crushes on anyone: I did. His name was Paul Kitt. He wore knickers, long socks, beautiful bulky sweaters and he always walked with his dog, an Irish setter. I used to hurry to walk behind him to school. He was great. His dad was a lawyer and I figured he had lots of money and I just loved him from afar. He didn't even know I was around. I'd ooh and aah about boys, because everyone else did, but actually I wasn't interested. As I remember back, Mom and Grandma always had something for me to do so I wasn't ever bored.

I don't believe I'd ever heard the word bored anyway. We didn't play the TV or radio unless Dad said we could, but there was lots of books and conversation, mostly with Grandma. I guess I daydreamed a lot too.

Someone decided that my brother should form a band and one day this fella drove up and took an accordion out of his car. His name was Lewis Edward Jones and he was from Avalon, Missouri. He lived with his dad in Kansas City. I found out he lived with his grandparents and he intended to go to Kansas City to school soon. Maybe I had a crush on him, but I don't think so. He was a lot older than me, but he kinda had nice eyes. He wasn't tall but he had a couple of bad habits. He drank too much and he had a bad temper. Well, I guess he must have worked some with my brother, but by this time, I was ready to leave for Kansas City myself, so I didn't think much about him.

After Grandma, I had been in the city for a while, I began to get invitations to go to the movies and maybe to go eat. Grandma always went along in the movies. She'd sit between me and whoever invited me. You must remember, as I do that at this point I'm beginning to think I'm a little too grown up for this. I wasn't, but I thought so. There were a couple of guys who wanted to date me, who were entertainers. One was Charlie Stewart. I guess he and I were engaged later five or six times over the years, but he drank too much too. The other was a really good looking boy, Frankie Kaye, who played the steel guitar.

Grandma definitely didn't like Charlie, although he was always nice to her and she didn't really care about Frankie, so my dating was extremely limited. Enter Lewis Jones, the old country boy. She, Grandma, didn't like him at all, no way, no siree. He drank too much and he didn't have a job. Grandma asked Millie to talk to me. She thought I was getting too close to Lewis and she was afraid I'd run off and marry him. Millie talked to me and at first it made me mad. But I was fifteen-going-on-twenty and I believed I'd do what I want too.

Off into forbidden territory I'd go with Lewis in his car. He'd tell me how much he didn't care about any women and in the next breath I'd hear that we should be together. No one had ever said anything like that to me. I wasn't used to being flattered or hearing anything like he was saying. Really I wanted to be my own person and get away from Grandma, and away from Kansas City.

I just wanted to be away and I'll be damned if I didn't say I was eighteen and we got married. No lights went off in my head, no bells rang, no music played. The next thing I knew I was fifteen years old with a good job at the radio station and married.

It was almost vacation time at the station, and by this time, we are being able to make transcriptions so on my wedding night I was at the station with Millie doing recording and Lewis was somewhere getting drunk and trying to figure out what he'd done. Millie noticed I was extremely nervous and she wanted to know what was wrong. I told her I'd married Lewis Jones that afternoon. I thought she was going to faint. The program director, Fran Allison came in and Millie told him. I think everyone came in and I really believed they were trying to console me and figure out a way to get me out of my predicament, and Lord knows, I was trying to figure out what to do myself.

No one had ever told me about married life or sex, what to do or not to do. I was really scared. The thing I was most scared of was Grandma. She had gone back to Chillicothe for business and she would be home that night on the bus.

She had always trusted me and believed in me and now without a thought of any consequences I'd gone off like a nut and got married. Maybe I'd let Millie explain, or maybe nobody would explain and I'd just drop dead, I always thought I'd die before I was twenty, anyway. What was I going to do before 8:30 that night when Grandma got in from Chillicothe? I must have turned deathly pale, 'cause someone got me a chair and some water. Then I heard Millie tell Fran, we couldn't continue until I felt better. I bet everyone thought I was pregnant, the way I acted, but I wasn't. I was feeling really terrible.

There wasn't anything to do but meet this head-on. That's what I decided at last. I'd meet the bus and just tell Grandma what happened and she'd understand. I'd never had anything to do with Lewis except kisses and he was twenty-seven and I was only fifteen so that would be grounds for something. Grandma was really going to be hurt, because we were about to move into a bigger apartment in Millie's building and things would be nicer and now I'd gone and messed everything up good! But at least I was on vacation. Doesn't that sound like a kid, finding something good in a situation?

My wedding night is one event I'll never forget. Lewis was drunk, Grandma was mad at me. I just didn't know which way to go, so I finally decided we should move over to the new apartment. I'd already paid the rent, so why not move in. There was only one bed in the old apartment. It folded up in the wall when you weren't using it and then you could have a small living room. The new place had a real bed and a real living room, with a little kitchen.

Grandma and I moved to the new place and Lewis stayed in the old place. Talk about comedy—that's what it looked like, me and Grandma on my wedding night.

I didn't tell you what Grandma said when Millie and I met the bus. Nothing, absolutely nothing! That meant trouble in itself. She'd let go sometime, I knew but when I didn't know. When she did, everyone better watch out. There wasn't anyone to blame but me, but everyone on earth was going to catch it—the radio station, Millie, me, and, most of all, Lewis. I figured if I'd get some sleep I could think better.

Up to now Lewis and I hadn't said a total of twenty words to one another. But in those twenty he said, "Honeymoon." He decided to take Grandma to Chillicothe then come back and get me and take me to Forsythe, Missouri in the Ozarks for our honeymoon. It was a nice idea but it turned into a total disaster. We were around lakes and water and lots of sun. I'm fair-skinned. I got the worst sunburn a human ever had and my body was blistered so bad I had to sleep on my stomach all the days we were there. Lewis just consumed a lot of beer and left me alone a lot. I really didn't care. The times I did get up I'd play the guitar a little and about this time I started to write songs. Tear-jerkers they're called now.

Lewis's father and stepmother considered all entertainers trash and no-goods. I never figured out why because I had a good job, was taking care of myself and Grandma and living pretty good. We weren't rich, but we were comfortable. The station had given me a raise and we did lots of personal appearances and for a woman to be earning seventy-five to eighty dollars a week in 1947 was really something.

I didn't know how to be married. I knew how to sing and entertain but I wasn't a wife. I think I tried but I just wasn't ready to be married. Lewis considered me a kid, not a woman. He told me, so things didn't get any better, they just got worse. He turned out to be not a nice person. I was gone most of the time, but when I was home things were bad. I'd seen Mom and Dad argue, but we went beyond arguing. Friday nights he'd buy five pounds of shrimp. He'd boil them with spices. He'd buy Italian olives and lots of beer. I didn't drink. I didn't drive a car until later and only then because he was drunk and I wanted to go home.

Saturday nights after the Brush Creek Follies we'd go to Chillicothe. He'd leave me at my folks and take off to find his old girlfriend and he wouldn't come back until Sunday night when we'd go back to the city. One night like that I had my dad take me down to her house and there they sat drinking beer. She had her arm around him and I opened the car door got a hold of her ponytail and dragged her out of the car. I didn't let go until I had whopped her good. I believe I said, "That's my car you're sitting in so get your ass out." At least that's what Dad said I said. I was telling the truth too.

In the years we were married I never saw a paycheck from Lewis. He was always going to school to be a watchmaker or something like that, but he never amounted to a whole lot.

I stayed with him because I thought when you got married that's what you did, no matter what. But what turned into beatings now and then and after almost four years I decided I wouldn't take anymore. I moved out. By this time I was driving. I took the car and went to Chillicothe, picked up Grandma and we moved into an apartment at the Washington Hotel not far from the radio station, which was located at 11th and Central.

So much for married life. I later went to Chillicothe and Mr. Bob Frith, my dad's lawyer, got me a divorce. I still had my job. I had Grandma. I had my Little Martin, which by now was nine years old and I was nineteen and single again.

This time with Grandma was quite different. I guess she saw I was really having a bad time from being divorced. She tried to tell me not to blame myself, that things would be better as time passed. I ended up leaving the radio station. For a few weeks I just went to pieces. Mr. Cupp and Millie thought it might be best for me to take a little time off so that's what I did. I went home to the folks and tried to regroup. I knew I wanted to be an entertainer but didn't necessarily want to be on the radio. I'd been there five years and I couldn't see me being there another five. Millie was content but I wasn't. Maybe I didn't want to be a part of a duet. I wanted to sing alone and have my own style. I worked on songs and different ways of singing them and worked up several different Yodel songs then I'd teach Millie.

I have to tell you one funny story. We sang a yodel song called "Love Knot in my Lariat." One line is when I swing my old lasso you'll hear my "Yodel-o." It didn't seem to be coming out the way we sang it. Mr. Cupp called us in his office and told us we'd have to quit singing it. Naturally I wanted to know why? He said listen to this and when he played the transcription it sounded like, "When I swing my old asshole." So we changed it to "Old Lassue." Every time we sang it we laughed.

Folks, it's high time you were properly introduced to *Millie* and *Sue*, our cute little hillbilly-singing girl team. Sue's the baby of our talent staff — just 18—and a fairly local product, having been raised in Chillicothe. *Millie* hails from Cross Timbers, Mo., down in the Ozarks, and the thing that amazes Jim is that these two little gals can their living sing-

MILLIE & SUE

ing when they never had any voice lessons, and playing guitar and mandolin when they never had any music lessons! Just naturally musical, that's all. Even taught themselves yodelling and cackle-singing! Matter of fact, *Millie* can play the fiddle, too, and *Sue* performs sometimes on the accordian. Lately they've taken up tap dancing and comedy routines, which they display Saturday evenings on the *Brush Creek Follies*. *Millie and Sue* have their own 15-minute show at 5:30 a. m. Monday through Saturday, and they're also on the *Dinner Bell Roundup Hour* at noon, weekdays. The gals have a wide fan following—recently Carol and Frances Bowersock, four-year-old twin daughters of the Justin D. Bowersocks of Kansas City, asked what they wanted for their birthday, responded in unison, "Millie and Sue." They got 'em, too. *Millie and Sue* arrived in time for the birthday cake—a highly appropriate one, since it happened to be *Sue's* birthday also. The twins were garbed like cowgirls for the occasion and everybody had a high old time. Yessir. KMBC can produce for you, whether it's radio entertainment or birthday surprises. But then, you already know that, if you stay with us at the 980 dial spot!

★ ★ ★

12:55-9 p. m. daily, KMBC-FM, 109.5 mc.

[Here's an article that appeared about me when I was eighteen]

The days of live radio had a million laughs, if you looked for them. Sometimes Hoby Schelp's bunch, after the engineer would cue them, would act like they were playing and singing and there would be just dead air. The engineer would be going crazy trying to find out what was wrong.

50

One time Paul Nesselroad, the news announcer, was reading the news and someone set fire to his script. He started out slow but I'll tell you he ended up fast. Down in the basement of KMBC they had lots of new equipment—something called television. We thought they were crazy trying to send your picture through the air. Turns out they weren't. Also they had their sister station KFRM which went out to western Kansas. We did a 1:00 show right after the Dinner Bell Roundup with Tiny Tillman. We came on the air one day and Tiny said, "Let's hurry up and get this abortion over with." Needless to say he was suspended for a few days till everyone got over that.

Mostly though those years I was growing up, and not in size. Don Sullivan tells me I was a little person when he first saw me at fourteen but I'm still a little person. I just got to five-two and never did go any further. I've still got one of my little outfits from radio days. A black satin skirt and jacket and we'd wear a white satin blouse and black cowboy hat and black boots. I guess we did look pretty good.

[Hoby Schelp]

[Hoby's group]

For about a year I had blond hair, probably because I thought I should, surely some kind of rebellion. It wasn't long until I knew I wasn't a blond but the same old redhead. Dad used to tease me when I was little and tell me my hair looked like a milo stock when it was ripe or a big old pumpkin. Then he'd laugh. I'd get mad inside, but then I'd laugh too, 'cause I thought the same thing. Anyway we all have to try something one time. How are you going to know what you like or don't like if you don't find out firsthand. My days of finding out what I liked were going to be coming around quickly.

What I liked was singing alone, doing comedy, like a younger Minnie Pearl, dressed in a feed sack and combat boots and having a good time entertaining. I don't mean to be ungrateful to Millie or any of my radio buddies, but I guess I must have had an ambition—not to be a star, just to be able to sing and make a good living. But now I was being faced with a change again. I wanted to hear different music and meet other musicians and find out how they felt about everything in general.

I've always been a curious person wanting to always know why this or that. Father Augustine my priest in Chillicothe, always tells me just to accept, Shirley, but that's really hard for me. When I finally do, then things seem better. Or if I turn things over to God, Thy will be done, whatever is bothering me works out. But at that time in my life I wasn't ready to turn things over to anyone but me. Bull-headed, stubborn, I believe it's called.

The separation and divorce from Lewis were more than traumatic to me. I felt if all marriages were like the one I had been in I didn't want any part of marriage again. So I began dating, which I really hadn't done before. I went with a Sicilian man from Kansas City, great-looking guy. He'd take me for spaghetti or lasagna or some of those good Italian foods but he made the mistake of taking me to meet his mother. She had a fit when she saw my red hair. She yelled something at him, I believe it was to get me out of her house and the romance was over for us.

Later he tried to patch things up and get together again. I was in Chillicothe and he came to my folks' house and my dad threw him out. How dare I go with a foreign person who didn't speak our language? I didn't know Dad was a bigot when it came to things like that but he was.

I loved dark-eyed, dark-haired men. I only married one and he was a Texan and maybe he did speak a foreign language—some of those Texans are hard to understand. Then as fate, would have it, I met the boy next door. Same birthday as mine, both Pisces people, same likes and dislikes, and we'd gone to school together. A romance made in Hell. Two people of the same sign definitely do not get along. You have to give me an "E" for effort. I had been learning. Not much about music but quite a bit about life. It was time to return to my first true love.

Getting Back to Music

My time with KMBC and Millie was just about to come to an end. I told her I'd just about decided to quit and go to Texas. We'd been there on a show and I really liked it. I talked to Grandma and asked her if she'd like a change. Naturally she said yes, she always liked change, so we decided to go to Corpus Christi, Texas. "To a place down by the sea, where contentment waits for me."

Catch the Breeze
Shirley Nelson

Once again it's time for flight.
So I'll spread my wings and fly.
To someplace down by the sea.
Where contentment waits for me.
Cause my spirit loves to roam.
Can't be confined within a home.
It must have the open air.
So I hurry to be there.

I must catch the breeze and fly.
I must catch the breeze and fly.
To someplace down by the sea.
Where contentment waits for me.
So I leave behind my dreams.
'Cause I have to travel light.
Can't let nothing weigh me down
When I catch the breeze and fly.
Up above the clouds so high.
Till I hear the ocean roar.
Then the sun will hit my face.
And I know I've found my place.

I must catch the breeze and fly.
I must catch the breeze and fly.
To someplace down by the sea.
Where contentment waits for me.
I must catch the breeze and Fly- I—I.

As I look back, I don't know if I'd be that secure in doing something like that, but I guess I wasn't thinking about security. Only "Pickin' and Singin'." So Grandma and I loaded up everything we had and took off for Texas. Now I'd never seen the ocean before, or seagulls, or a sea wall, so I was completely in awe of the whole works. We found a little house out near the Navy Base at Flour Bluff on Padre Island. I don't remember what the rent was but I can bet you it was cheap.

Grandma didn't have much to say about the change except that it sure was hot. I began right away finding out what was going on. In the music business and where did I, could, find a place to play. I will say that I had a lot of determination or guts. I'd just walk up to a bandstand and tell them I sang and I'd like to sit in. Nothing like being straightforward, is there?

Usually they let me. I don't remember being refused. Sometimes bands won't let anyone sit in. First of all people don't know the key you sing in or they sing one song and want you to sing all night. Being a woman and walking up to a bandstand in the early '50s was being pretty gritty. This one band I settled on was Al Hardy and the Westerners. I really bugged him to let me try out for him. Finally I did and afterward he told me, "I really like your singing but I don't need another singer, I need a bass player." I guess I figured I'd better start looking someplace else so I left. The chances of working for him didn't seem very good. Al was a great big man, truly Texas. Later I learned he'd been in the cavalry and he loved horses, jokes and that he had a heart of gold. So did his wife Mary.

Anyway, the next day a car drove up outside our door opened and Al put a Fender electric bass and amp inside, he looked at me and said, "Learn to play this and come to work tonight." The door closed and I just sat there, bewildered. My first thought was, "What just happened, and the next was, "Do it."

The Little Martin and I went to work. I would play chords on the Little Martin, then pick up the bass and find out where the chord was, and then I'd play the bass notes. I went to work that night. After the dance I asked Al, "How did I sound."

He said, and I remember his exact words, "You sure can sing, but your bass playing stinks."

Just a few months later he wouldn't be able to say that again, because people would be coming to hear me play. I was the only women bass player in the city of Corpus Christi, Texas. Al told me something else I didn't realize either. He had insight into presenting a song and one night I was standing playing and singing some kind of boogie-woogie thing and he told me it sounded like a ballad. Also how in the world could I sing a song about a no-good-dirty cheating rat and smile about it? Food for thought, so I thought about it. How could I?

At this time in my life I began to listen to what I was saying. It's difficult to get your feelings across in a dance hall when the people are interested in dancing, drinking and partying but somehow I managed, and they began to listen and come to see us.

I've never had too many problems with the other musicians but in Corpus Christi I had one. The guy who played bass before me for Al, and then was let go because of me, used to come out to our shows and really give me a bad time about causing him to lose his job. He was really bitter toward me. I didn't mean him any harm at all. I just needed a good job and he already had a job at the Naval Base and played extra, so when he began to see I was really serious about needing the job and that I was turning into a pretty good bass player. Eventually he sort of slacked off. Other than that I didn't have much trouble.

There was a slow time just after I'd gone to work with Al and he, Al, suggested I try to pick up some other jobs. One was at a club called the Blue Moon or some kind of moon near Padre Island. I was playing an upright bass there. I'm not sure if they even had electricity, and the bridge broke which let the strings do a loud pop.

As this was not the best club in the world, I think everybody carried a gun except me. So when the bridge broke our fiddle player dove out of the little window in the back of the bandstand. I guess he figured there was some jealous husband after him. Anyhow he did a roll out the window, and when he came up all he had left was the strings and the keys all the rest was gone. Quite a funny sight.

By this time my old car had almost given out and when I'd be driving I'd smell something burning. It only had one gear in it, straight ahead, so if you wanted to turn around you had to go where you could drive in a circle. One night as I was playing some people came in and told me my car was on fire. I just said, "Let it burn." And it sure did. When I got through playing I went outside and all that was there was the frame. It looked like a cartoon sketch. If you blew on it, it would fade away. I just laughed and caught a ride home to Grandma. Al helped me get another car, not fancy at all, but at least I could get to work. *

During this time Grandma didn't say too much about the situations we were in. I knew things had to get worse to get better. I did have a job but we sure were a long way from Missouri. When we'd left Missouri, I had left the radio station with good feelings and I knew I could go back. Millie was just doing a solo act so I didn't think it would be hard to go back there to work. The only trouble was I didn't want to have to do that. I still had my Little Martin and Grandma and I could sing and play and I knew somewhere I could make a living for us.

By then I was twenty my guitar was ten and I believe Grandma must have been somewhere over sixty. Isn't that funny, I always thought Grandma was ageless. She was never old or would never grow old to me. When I'd go play at the clubs she commanded a table by the bandstand and if anyone wanted to have coffee with me or talk to me you had to see my grandma first. She screened everyone I met.

Once again my love life was on hold. Believe it or not I didn't have time to think of being in love, though I was a few times during the couple of years we stayed there. One was with a commander in the Navy. I think he must have reminded me of Paul Kitt, who I had a crush on in my early life, 'cause he had an Irish setter that rode around with him all the time. But he fell into the swimming pool at the naval base when the pool was empty and he broke both arms. Then shortly after that he was shipped out. So much for navy life. Another man I was interested in was J. R. Baker, a good-looking, dark-complected, black haired, guitar-playing Texan; And Grandma didn't like him at all because he was a Cherokee Indian. When he'd come over she'd go in her room with her detective books and she wouldn't come out. I was learning bigotry. I don't mean learning to be a bigot, but I was learning not to be one.

I was like Dad. When someone said no I always said yes. But that romance didn't last long either. Al Hardy didn't like him any more than Grandma did and threatened not to let him work with us if I didn't quit seeing him.

How in the world I saw him anytime is beyond me. We worked from 8:30 to midnight, then I would go to an after-hours club from one to four A.M., then go out and eat or out to Padre Island to see the sun come up. I'd sit in my car right on the ocean's edge and just try to understand who I was and what I was doing. I felt like a little four-year-old girl sitting on the front steps at 1100 Locust in Chillicothe, trying to figure out what and who I was.

It's very strange. I always felt that I'd been born to the wrong family. Not Grandma of course but I felt that God placed me down among a bunch of people I didn't know. When I went back home at thirty-nine years old, I had the same feeling. And today at seventy-five I still feel that way. I guess I shouldn't question so much.

Things in Texas were going better. Grandma and I had a house off Ocean Drive and a better car and more money. We, Al and the band, had a TV show for Yarborough Coffee and I was their spokesperson. The first time I held the coffee cup it rattled so badly I started laughing, then I held it with both hands. We became very successful and probably the most popular band around Corpus.

I need to tell you a funny story about moving from Flour Bluff or why we moved. The house burned. So that's reason enough but the way it burned was funny. I had come home from playing. I was by myself. Grandma had gone back to Chillicothe for a while. Anyway I just had gotten to sleep when I heard someone yelling, "Get the children out and anything valuable." I was so laid-back nothing fazed me. These people, whoever they were, were carrying out this old furniture we had like I wasn't even there. Very casually I asked what was wrong. A woman told me the back of the house was on fire and I'd better get out. Someone had called the fire department from the naval base and they were on their way.

By the time the fire department got there and put out the blaze it just exploded. Again the fire went up. Well, they decided a gas well was underneath my hot water heater and had a leak, and they would have to get a map and shut it off. I got so tired standing outside with my guitar and pocketbook. So I went inside and made a pot of coffee. All at once I heard this tapping on the back porch and I opened the door. It was a fireman. Naturally, I asked him if he'd like a cup of coffee. His eyes got real wide and he said, "Get yourself out of this house, it might explode anytime." I bet I looked ridiculous with my guitar, pocketbook and a coffee pot standing out in the front yard. Well, what was I supposed to do but be calm?

One of the people who owned a club where the band worked was in the crowd and offered Grandma and me the house off Ocean Drive. Good things do come along at odd times. The way I place value is strange, because another time after I'd gotten back to Chillicothe in 1970 the diesel tank down the street had sprung a leak and loudspeakers were going up and down the street telling everyone to take what they valued and leave. I took my little poodle, Toby, my purse, and of course my little guitar.

That guitar has never ever been more than a few feet away from me even when I sleep. I used to keep it under the bed or almost always by the bed. I'm a very light sleeper and sometimes to get myself calmed down or if I wake up from dreaming I can play a little bit and I'll go back to sleep. Same case, same keys, same body. Nothing has ever been changed.

Here Comes Change Again

The Little Martin was ten years old and I was twenty. Grandma wanted to have a serious talk, and when she said that, she meant it. All attention was the order of the day. She was going to go back to Chillicothe and try to get some welfare benefits. She was going to leave me alone and "For Pete's sake, don't go doing anything silly, like marrying somebody," she told me.

She really felt it would be best for us to go back to Missouri. I really didn't know why she felt that way but she did. She wanted me to think things over and see how I felt before she came back. In other words I think she was asking me if I was content in playing clubs for the rest of my life. No way was that gonna happen. So I started to think, there's got to be something better, and before she'd been home three days she called me. She told me Mom said Red Foley had a new television show from Springfield, Missouri every Saturday and I should come home and get on it.

It was so simple to them and simple to me at the time. You know you just walk in and say here I am, haven't you been waiting on me. Well, it didn't quite work like that. First I had to get back to Chillicothe. I didn't have very many possessions, so that wasn't going to bog me down. I had acquired a canary, a red roller, so I wasn't going to leave him, and one of my romances had given me the cutest Pekingese dog, I named him Rusty, and a few clothes. I told everybody goodbye, gave Al back his bass, loaded up my car with the few things I had and started to Chillicothe.

I believe it's about fifteen-hundred miles, but to me it was the longest trip I'd ever made alone. I'd ride along, sing, the bird would sing, the dog would howl, we'd stop a few minutes. Those events occurred all the way to Missouri. I sure hoped everyone was right that I would get a job on the Ozark Jubilee.

I didn't know who to call to see about an audition, so I decided the best thing was to just take my guitar and go down to Springfield. So Mom and my sister, Mary, and I made the trip. I knew the show was at the Jewel Theater, so we just walked in. They were having rehearsals and I believe I talked to Si Siman first and asked him if he'd listen to me sing. I did "I Betcha My Heart I Love You," a yodel song and something else but I don't remember what it was. Most all the cast members were out in the theater and they gave me a nice round of applause when I got through. But nobody said you're hired. Si came up to me and told me they all liked what I did, he said I should go back to Chillicothe and they'd let me know. Sounds like KMBC again, doesn't it? Don't call us, we'll call you.

And call me they did. It took a few days but Si called. He told me I should come on down and start on the Eddy Arnold Show which was televised on Thursday evenings. Was I ever excited! The strings on the little guitar were as happy as I was, when started practicing a few songs.

Do you know I didn't ask what I'd be paid or if I was really hired or any of the important things, but a chance to be with Eddy Arnold was terrific. I'd listened to his records and heard him on the radio and seen him on television and I was put on cloud nine.

Now I had to decide what to wear. After I left KMBC, I always wore skirts and pretty blouses. I had a good figure and I preferred something simple, not flaky. I had gotten a chance to see the Jubilee and I noticed that it wasn't all that flashy either. So I thought I was probably on the right track. As far as make-up, I didn't use too much of anything on my face. I had a nice complexion and so I just let my face hang out there for everyone to see.So, onward to Springfield! This time I went by myself. Why Grandma didn't go along. I'm not too sure about why. She hadn't been feeling all that well. She had diabetes and sometimes that made her feel bad. It could have been that money was awfully tight and there was only enough for me to make the trip. But I do know the difference between this job and my audition in Kansas City. This time I was not afraid! I had gained a little in confidence and knew I had the ability to entertain. Just give me a chance, that's all I needed. I'd been on television in Texas so I figured this wouldn't be too different from there. What I had laughed about in the late '40s was now being broadcast everywhere. Sending pictures through the air really happened, and to think I'd seen all this equipment before a lot of people had. So onward to Eddy's show.When I got there and met him he was so nice you just wouldn't believe it. This television was going to be quite a bit different because we had sets and camera rehearsal and music rehearsal. We just didn't go in like in Texas and start playing. I loved challenges and change so I'm all for everything. Eddy and I did a little skit together that night on his show. I was the teacher teaching him his ABCs and he was the pupil, school desk and all. We sang "A, You're Adorable." I'd sing the letters and he'd finish with the words quite a clever song. Later I yodeled "I Betcha My Heart" and the audience seemed to really like me.As far as television was concerned I didn't worry about the camera. I let the camera worry about me. I was entertaining and loving every minute of it. As far as I knew I hadn't been accepted for the Jubilee, but that night at the show Eddy announced I would become a regular on the Ozark Jubilee beginning Saturday. That meant I had to get back to Chillicothe, get some more clothes, find a place to live and begin again. But as long as I had Grandma I'd be fine. From the Saturday on I'd be on nationwide television, singing by myself, doing my own thing and getting paid twenty-five dollars a show. People think we made more, but we didn't. That's okay. It was just me and the Little Martin doing things our way. I felt maybe I was on the right road after all.

My name now became Shirley Caddell. I had gone to school with a man named Bill Caddell and the people at the station thought Caddell sounded better than Jones, which had been my married name.

I was twenty-one years old and my best friend, my guitar was eleven. We had a whole lot of living to do, and did we ever live it. Needless to say everyone at home was pretty excited about me going to be on television. You must remember television was still somewhat new and everyone who was anyone watched it. It's still amazing to me! But to me I guess I was only thinking I had a job again, where maybe I could finally do what I wanted to as far as singing. But I had a few things to learn.

The first thing I learned was the director Bryan Bissley, thought it was not feminine for a girl to play a guitar on TV. The news hit me like a bomb, the Little Martin and I had always been together on every show except when I was playing bass and now she wouldn't be on TV. What a blow. But you know, Wanda Jackson from Oklahoma visited a few times on the Jubilee, and she always played her guitar, and then I made a little fuss. It really didn't do much good but I did it anyway. So the Little Martin was on several times.

We had two bands who worked with Red Foley, Grady Martin who I absolutely adored, and Bill Wemberly, who I believe in my heart was nuts. He believed, and this is my opinion, in doing everything the wrong way. For instance, I was on the road a couple of days with him and the band, we were stopped by the state patrol and lo and behold he was running a car license on his bus. I guess we all laughed but we probably thought about how to get to Springfield from where ever we were.

He had a terrific band, Thumbs Carlyle. He played the guitar with it laying down on his lap. He was really into drugs, what kind I don't know. But he was a great musician, so we overlooked whatever he was doing.

Jimmie Belken, I adored him too, a wonderful fiddle player. I didn't know at the time but for the rest of my life I'd be meeting this man, somewhere, with Bob Wills, with Merle Haggard, and several others I can't remember. Jimmie told me the last time I saw him, that he had beat the big "C" thanks to St. Jude, and also that we'd met so much. He wondered why we didn't get married. Now I see him on television with Merle and I'm sure I'll be seeing him somewhere else when I least expect it. But the band I kind of leaned toward to was Grady's. He was such a great musician, that again I was in awe of him.The only way I was going to make any money at the Jubilee was by working on the road, so Grady decided to use me on some of his jobs but Bill decided to use me some too. With Grady you rode in his car, he drove like a maniac. With Bill you never knew what to expect. So truly I was in the best of both worlds. I don't believe I was scared of anything. These bands, Grady's and Bill's alternated week to week. So sometimes we might not be on television. Or sometimes I would be booked somewhere out yonder, mostly back east.I'd never had any dealings with a booking agency, but I found an awfully nice friend in the booker at the Jubilee, Lucky Moeller and Lou Black. Its agency was top talent. What nice guys! I can remember going up to their office and asking them why I wasn't on the Red Foley Tours. I don't believe I got an answer. They'd just book me somewhere else. You know I think I told you a story about never having a booker before, because I did have a booking agent in Kansas City, KMBC had its own booker. Jimmy McConnell. I'm truly sorry because he was a great person. Maybe the difference here is, I dealt with Lucky myself and Millie and the station had more to say where I was going than I did, due to my age probably.

Let me get back to Grady. His life at the Jubilee was going to be short, due to some difficulties with Red. One night I drove out to Grady's and Red was chasing Grady around the house, then they'd turn and Grady would be chasing Red and I believe it ended up with Red getting hit in the head with a fiddle. I'd rather not say what the fight was about, but it wasn't a pretty picture. Shortly after that Bill became the band for Red. Of course we had Slim Wilson and his band, Porter Waggoner, Speedy Haworth, Don Warden, Harold Morrison and Jimmy Gately, so we weren't shy on musicians. We had all kinds of people on the show.

Later when Webb Pierce and I became good friends, Chuck Bowers would always be around. He was a great singer. Webb, Chuck and myself, Jimmy Gately and Harold Morrison, a couple of good ol' musicians who'd made it to the Jubilee and would still be there when I left, a part of our family of entertainers, had a fifteen-minute TV Show on KYTV 3 in Springfield for the Biederman furniture store.One night we did a personal appearance in a little town not far from Springfield. This elderly couple came up to me and said that they got dressed up every night and got in front of the TV. She said, "Don't you think we always look nice." Naturally I figured she thought we saw them when they saw us, so I just smiled and said, "You always look nice." She was so happy.

TV did weird things to people. To some people TV gave big egos—to others it was just a job. Most of the regulars at the Ozark Jubilee I think just saw it as a job. Once when several of us began to think twenty-five dollars wasn't enough per show, I became the spokes person to speak to Si Siman. Si told me that by rights we should be paying them for all the exposure. So I told him would he please tell my landlady that? I think we both laughed. But he might be right. I knew the Grand Ole Opry didn't pay anything either. I believe Ernest Tubb told me he was paid more than anyone and that was only fifty dollars.

Jean Shepherd was still at the Ozark Jubilee when I got there. I had seen a show with Red and her when he introduced her he said, "This little girl is really going to be big-time someday." Now like a dream when he introduced me he would almost always say, "I really wish we had color TV. This little lady has the most beautiful red hair I've ever seen." What an introduction. You know I loved to sing with him too.

I became known at the Jubilee for being able to sing with anybody. It didn't make any difference who you were I could sing harmony. I believe it's just something about my voice that blends with others or it could be I just like to sing harmony. This takes me back to school days when I'd go to early morning choir practice before school. Mrs. Sawyer, that's Mrs. True Sawyer, would say to me sing this alto part, or sing this soprano part, or sing this alto tenor part, or sing the bass part. Some kid wouldn't show up and I'd have to sing their part. But it didn't make any difference to me, I was singing.

But at the Jubilee, I did have chances to sing with Jimmie Wakely, Webb Pierce, Rex Allen, who taught me a little about TV. He, Rex, made it a special point to sit me down and make me understand that what the camera saw was limited. When I tossed my head around, like I sometimes did, especially when I was yodeling, my face would go clear off the screen. So I had to learn to sing to the camera. I thought the camera would do all the work, but you definitely should help it.I guess for an early fifties TV show, the Jubilee really wasn't all that great in production. But at the same time it had some of the best talent around anywhere. I had a chance to look at some of the old clips and see myself again after all these years and the sets consisted mainly of a rail fence or a bale of straw a chair or wagon wheel or something really primitive. The way country was coming across then was not the slick country it is now. No sequins or tight dresses or low-cut gowns. But I didn't wear them anyway. I didn't wear cowboy boots either, or a cowboy hat like I had at KMBC.Things were changing again and all for the better. There were so many people coming to that show it was really unbelievable. Carl Perkins was one, with his hit "Blue Suede Shoes." In fact the night when he finished the show was the same night he had his terrible wreck that almost ended his career. Johnny Horton was there too, with his song, "The Battle of New Orleans." He was a wonderful, wonderful person. I remember talking to him and he told me he felt everything for him was right and his star was on the rise. Not too long after that conversation Johnny was coming in from a show and his car crashed.

Then there was Johnny Cash, a young man who appeared with us, when I finally did get to do a Red Foley tour, in San Antonio, Texas. Everyone was flabbergasted at his style, how very different from anything we'd ever heard. That difference is what makes his music so great to this day.

On the Red Foley road show, I'd go out, do three numbers, and then everybody would come back at the end to sing "Shake a Hand." That was Red's closing number.

You know I don't remember was I was paid, but I do remember I was getting along all right so I'd say the pay was good. During this time, Grandma didn't come to Springfield to live with me. I was gone so much, and I didn't feel it was right for her to be alone. So she stayed in Chillicothe, but Mom and Grandma and Mary Lou would be down once in awhile and when I had a day or two off I'd go up to see them.

Charlie Hodge of the Foggy River Boys had an MG car and I just about had a fit over it, I wanted a car so bad. I finally got a '53 white Corvette just right after they came out and probably drove it a dozen times. This guy I was going with was going to take care of it while I was in Pennsylvania. He had taken me to the airport in Kansas City and when I finally got a hold of him from Pennsylvania he told me he'd had a little trouble. The little trouble was he'd hit something and with that fiberglass body they had then it just broke apart. The poor headlights popped right out. It was a terrible sight. I didn't get mad or scream or anything like that. I simply never spoke to him or saw him again.

A few years later when I was on television in California, I got a call from Charlie Hodge, who by then was with Elvis—he was the little guy who always handed Elvis his scarves. He said, "Elvis loves you, Shirley. Would you yodel for him?" What a thrill, Elvis watching me. He liked "Quits" too, a comedy character I did. But you'll hear about her later.So, back to the Jubilee. One Saturday when Webb was guest host, we were standing backstage and TV *Guide* wanted to photograph him for the cover. He said, "I want this girl in the picture, too," and grabbed hold of me. So I was going to be in TV *Guide* with Webb. I thanked him, of course. He said, "You know, Shirley, I'm going to get you a record contract." I just said O.K. I don't believe I was impressed.Up to that time I've never worked with a record out, but that's what he said he was going to do and three days later he called and said, "I want you to fly to Nashville and record for ABC Paramount." I'd never flown before. I'd never recorded before and I was overcome. Hello world, it's time for change again.My first airplane ride was very exciting to me. I didn't know how much I loved to fly. It was a prop plane and the stewardess could see I was a little apprehensive about flying so she calmed me down. I had called to tell Grandma I was flying to Nashville to record, and her response was the age-old statement I'd heard before—if God intended you to fly, Shirley, he would have given you wings. I checked, I didn't have wings, but I was flying anyway. When you're up in the air there is a certain sense of freedom. Over the years I would be flying so much from the Jubilee that I began to know the stewardesses and pilots so you might find me in the cabin visiting or if I'd be especially tired the girls would take the middle bar on the seat out and I'd go to sleep.

I was always treated super on planes. I just figured different than Grandma, I was closer to God when I got up there in the sky. I said I was a dreamer, didn't I? I believe Wayne Walker, a very talented songwriter in Nashville, met my plane and took me into town. I was staying at the James Robertson Hotel. The publishing company that Webb was a partner in was just up the street, within walking distance, where I'd be picking the songs I wanted, or they wanted me to sing. I'm not going to tell you I was very crazy about what I sang. In fact the only song I remember doing on ABC Paramount was "Where Did the Sunshine Go":

Where did the sunshine go?
Why is it raining so?
Where is the love I used to know?
Where did the sunshine go?

I had a pretty successful record on it anyway. So that was all that mattered. In later years Willie would tell me that song was one of his favorites. So I guess he was following me there. In fact, he did come to the Jubilee while I was there, Billy Walker brought Willie in to audition and they, Si Siman and Mr. Foster, wouldn't hire him. They said he was a little far out. That's probably not the term they used. But in those days he would have been considered far out. I heard later after they didn't hire him, he and Martha and the kids stayed in Springfield while he bussed tables at some restaurant there. When they had enough money, he took them on to Nashville. Our paths would be crossing, Willie's and mine, but we still hadn't met. Fate hadn't stepped in yet. I could see that country music was on the rise even then. Things had changed so much since KMBC Radio Days, though believe it or not it was still very difficult for women in the entertainment business. It was probably difficult everywhere but I just didn't know about it. The Jubilee was a star-studded show of those days. We had entertainers from everywhere. One in particular I remember was Dorothy Collins, from the Hit Parade Show in New York. I even remember what she sang—"Tell Me Why"—a beautiful love song. I was part of the scene she had sitting or standing around on camera listening to her sing.

Dorothy told me something that I've never forgotten. Why me, I don't know, but she told me, "A person should always be in love." She said she always was and that's what made her happy. I suppose I was searching in a usual way for something or somebody, but I didn't realize it. Maybe she just sensed that, too. But at the time I think I thought she meant you should be in love with someone, and I figured too, she must be pretty busy if she's always in love. I didn't know if I had time. Now when I think of that statement I realize how right she was. You must first love yourself and what you're doing and show that love to everyone around you. You don't necessarily have to be in love with another person, just love what God has created for you and everything will work out.

A friend of mine, Patsy Parcenski of Illinois calls me a caretaker and a God-sent friend. There are powerful words but that's the way she sees me. I only hope I can always live up to what people see. Anyway, our cast of people became a Who's Who of celebrities for those days—and I was right in the middle of them. Our regular cast featured Slim Wilson and his band, Lenny and Goo Goo—a comedy team, Uncle Cyp and Aunt Sap, a man and wife comedy team, Tabby West—another girl singer, Jimmy Gately, Harold Morrison, Chuck Bowers, Pete Stamper, Marvin Rainwater, Brenda Lee, the Matthews Brothers, The Promenaders, a square dance group of cute kids, Porter Wagoner, the original Foggy River Boys, Wanda Jackson, Bobby Lord, and Bill Ring.

A very funny story concerns Uncle Cyp, a great country comedian. Porter Wagoner, Speedy Haworth, his guitar player, Don Warden, his steel player, myself, Billy Walker and Uncle Cyp took off after the Jubilee on Saturday night, first to play in Denver,

Colorado, then back to Scottsbluff, Nebraska the next night. On the way Uncle Cyp started coughing and with five others in the car, I didn't say bus, I said car, it was really unbearable. Billy Walker and I threw barbs at one another, Porter would sing, then we'd all sing and Uncle Cyp would still cough. Nobody was able to even close an eye for a cat nap.

Knowing me, I told Porter whenever you stop this car I'm going to get Uncle Cyp something for that cough. If I don't I'm going crazy. Well, I went crazy until Denver and when we took off the next day for Scottsbluff I finally made him stop at a drugstore somewhere out there, cause Uncle Cyp was still coughing. I went in and got a bottle of Turpin Hydrate and gave it to Uncle Cyp to sip on. Well, the cough began to stop and by the time we got to Scottsbluff, Uncle Cyp couldn't even get out of the car. He had drunk the whole bottle. No one had bothered to tell me he was on the edge of being an alcoholic. Right then I had him over the edge.

I had always smelled a funny odor when I was around him and Aunt Sap. I later found out that it was formaldehyde. They sometimes give this to alcoholics to taper off. So much for my doctoring.

Finally, we made it back to Kansas City, Porter and Uncle Cyp and I bailed out at the airport and took the plane on to Springfield. I think I slept a couple of days after that. What a trip. Uncle Cyp called the stewardesses hostages and Porter and I had more than one laugh on that flight.

Porter Wagoner, a butcher from West Plains, Missouri who at first couldn't even say anything on a show, was by then one of the best talkers in Nashville. I always teased him and called him the white Nat "King" Cole. He'd let his hair get real white and then get a deep tan, and he was tall, like Nat was, so that was the reason I gave him the nickname. He just laughed and Porter always liked to laugh. If we ran out of things to do while we were traveling we always had time to laugh.

Most country entertainers can find something funny in almost anything. I used to travel quite a lot with another entertainer from the

Jubilee, Marvin Rainwater; I'm not really sure if he was an Indian or not, but he dressed like one and he had a big hit, "Gonna Find Me a Bluebird."

Let him sing me a song
'Cause my heart been broken much too long.
Gonna chase me a rainbow
To the heaven of blue,
'Cause I'm all through crying over you.

He and I would hit the road to Pennsylvania mostly by air, not the road. We did lots of country fairs up there. One in particular I'm thinking of was out from Harrisburg, Pennsylvania. We did the show and the crowd was almost all Amish people. They walked around eating French fried potatoes dipped in vinegar and they didn't applaud at the show until everyone had finished. I don't remember them laughing either, but they probably did. Anyhow Marvin did his part and as I recall he had some pretty funny stories to tell and when no one did anything, that is they didn't applaud, he got very upset. When we were back on the plane, he told me he wasn't coming back up there anymore. We were all buckled in ready to go, the fog rolled in on us and Marvin and I had to get off the plane. The airport said they would not be taking off and he just stomped around mad as could be.

We didn't take off the next morning, or evening, or the next or the next. We were there for almost a week and the only thing playing at the local movie house all week was "Moby Dick." I began to think Gregory Peck was a friend of mine, I'd seen him so much.Later on in California when I was on "The Groucho Marx Show" I was ashamed I didn't know the questions about Moby Dick, that's for sure. Anyway, I toughed it out, but the last day Marvin rented a car and drove us to the next date he was playing. He was a very funny man in all states but Pennsylvania. I liked Pennsylvania myself. I thought it was very pretty. I saw many, many states from the air or his window so it was difficult at times to really know too much about anyplace.

My life had become busy and trying to work enough to make a good living was sometimes difficult. I didn't have a lot of possessions, not like I do now.

I'm an accumulator. Nowadays, I hardly ever throw away anything in case I might need it someday. But then I threw away everything. I always had a furnished apartment with a little kitchen, not that I cooked that much, but sometimes I did want something different, and when I did go to Chillicothe, Grandma would make me everything she could think of. I loved her homemade tomato-potato soup and once again she'd get me with hot apple dumplings.

I didn't seem to gain a lot of weight. I just got to one place and kind of held that. No one at the Jubilee ever told me I was too heavy, and in the clips I see now I wasn't, but something strange was going on with me. I really wanted to belong to someone special.

Up to this time it was just fine, as I've told you, to have my music, my entertainer friends and work. But I knew out there in the real world there were parties and places to go and things to do. When we'd ride along in the bus after I joined the Phillip Morris show and I'd see people's homes with all the lights on it made me sad inside, and inside myself I wished for a sink full of dirty dishes.

Later in New York an advertising lady for Phillip Morris would write an article about my wish. I know I just wanted a home and family, maybe to place some roots for myself. But that would be a long time coming. Every time I went on the road my buddy and best friend, the Little Martin went with me. By this time the airlines knew she was to sit with me. Back then I didn't have to put her in the baggage compartment. She could be close all the time. She played to lots of people while we were at the Jubilee, maybe not appearing on TV only several times, but to those out in the states where we worked she always did her part. In the car she had a good place to ride. In the trunk she was comfortable with clothes piled around her to keep her from wobbling around, and do you know to this day she has never broken a string on me in any performance I have ever done. I just realized that. My other guitar a D-18 Martin would like to get me somewhere in the middle of a song and break an "E" string. You can't play with only five strings so you can bet your boots I left that guitar at home. Besides the Little Martin and I were buddies forever. She understood me.

Some years later after I was back with my folks, I felt I needed to get away for a couple days at a time. The only way anyone could tell I was really gone would be to look under the bed and see if Little Martin was gone. If she was, I was. I guess this really applies more after Willie and I separated and I lived back with my folks for a while. Mom would come to my apartment upstairs get down and look under the bed and tell Dad, she's left everything else, she'll be back, but the Little Martin is gone. There I was again taking the only thing I valued the most, my guitar, "my Little Martin."

Time for Fun

The Jubilee was a lot of fun-filled days, but also a lot of hard work. Everybody needs a relaxing time. Now everyone goes to Hawaii or Aspen, but in those days, where could a person go that was on a very limited income. Well I'm about to tell you where I went. This is really ridiculous, I was almost twenty, and I went to the circus for a month. I was leaving the Jewel after rehearsal and I had to go across the street to the drugstore. As I stepped off the curb, a car almost ran over me. When I looked up I saw a most handsome man was driving. Black hair and dark eyes and when he stopped the car and got out he was not only handsome, he was tall dark and handsome. He apologized to me and told me he was with the Gill Gray Shrine Circus and would I like to see the show. Here we are standing in the middle of the street and he's almost run over me and we're chatting like old friends.So I took the tickets, called one of the girls at KWTO Radio and asked her if she'd like to go to the circus that evening. We went and I told her how I came by the tickets. She thought that was great. It turned out Larry Cardin was a teeterboard artist, actually a catcher for them. That's the person who catches everyone on his shoulders. Sometimes he'd miss but not too often. He was with the Bobby Alexander group. Bobby is the person who teaches the people on "Circus of the Stars" in Hollywood. He also did most of the work on the great movie "Trapeze" with Burt Lancaster, Tony Curtis and Gina Lollobrigida. He did a lot of circus work with a black wig and ladies tights on and everyone at the circus teased him.

I want you to know I didn't fall in love with Larry. I needed to get away from all this work and traveling and see what was going on in someone else's world. Larry asked me to come along with the circus for a little while if I could get away. He had a travel trailer and I could make myself at home and enjoy traveling around with them. Enjoy traveling? This was going to be different. I thought about it, asked if I could be off the show for a while and got the okay from Si

Siman, so off I go into the wild, wild world of circus life. I met Larry in St. Joseph, Missouri. In fact I met the whole circus. They just treated me like I was one of the family. Naturally the Little Martin came along to entertain if necessary. Circus people are very different from music people. Still no one is entertaining but I believe it takes a lot more to be circus folks. They're always practicing and seeing what stunts they can do better, and believe me the little time I was with them you could always see bruises and marks on someone from all the extra knocks they take. When Larry would miss a catch off the teeterboard his shoulders would pay for it and his muscles ached all the time.

In later years I had an occasion to ask him about someone who knew him and they told me he died. He had Muscular Dystrophy. Probably it was coming on when I knew him. He and another guy they called "Red" did a clown act on the trampoline that was pretty dangerous too. Well I traveled around with them for about three weeks and in Fargo, North Dakota, they were practicing and Bobby looked at me and said, "You're about the right size to do teeter-board."

His wife and another very cute girl in the act had already taught me style. That's what you do when you finish your act or when someone has performed. You put one arm on your hip and the other arm goes into the air and it certainly has to be graceful. Anyway they were going to try for a three-man high and a small girl on top. So Bobby hooked me in a harness. This attaches to the top of the tent and if you miss your catch or you roll the harness catches you and doesn't let you fall. On the circus of the stars I see he Bobby uses this most of the time, so no one gets hurt.

Here I was the Jubilee's performer and all-around harmony singer strapped into a harness about to make my flight for life. The only thing I knew was if I didn't make it I wouldn't fall, and I didn't make it. When I went up into the air I could hear Grandma say again, "If God had wanted you to fly he'd given you wings." I checked again. No wings. All I wanted was down.

They all laughed, which made me feel better. No one ever puts anyone down as far as I could see with circus people. They may not like what you do but they will always build your confidence. I could tell at that moment I wasn't a circus performer and I really didn't think I'd look good in tights so I figured I better go back to what I knew, music.

Larry was going back to Springfield for a while, the circus had a break of some kind, and I told him I'd better get back to work. I think it was good experience, I wouldn't take anything for the time I spent or the people I met, I liked the midgets best they were so cute. But after all I was still a country music girl in a foreign world. So Little Martin and I were back on firm ground. Larry and I never made any commitment to one another. He did tell me that he wished we got married, but I didn't believe that was, the kind of life I wanted. He even drove up by my folk's house and asked them to talk to me. They really didn't think that was my world either but they met him and they did speak to me. But when I looked at Grandma I heard "NO FLYING."

Back to Work

Back at the Jubilee things were progressing at breakneck speed. They were getting bigger and bigger. Now when Red wanted to vacation a little we had great hosts. Still Webb Pierce, who would keep up to date on my recording, Sonny James, "The Southern Gentleman," and a perfectionist rolled into one, Tex Ritter, my hero, from Saturday matinee movies in Chillicothe. Can you imagine how I felt when I saw some of these people in person? I was so star struck it was pitiful.

The first time I saw Tex Ritter, Red Foley, Dub Allbritton, Red's Manager, and I went by a motel in Springfield to pick up Tex to go to a personal appearance. Dub knocked on the door and there stood my hero, in boots, underwear and his cowboy hat. He was a little tipsy but that didn't matter to me. He was still my hero. He always treated me nice. He called me little lady and he'd look in my eyes and make me feel like I was the only person on earth. I told him how many times my brother and I had spent our dime to see him at the movies and he was really grateful. He wasn't anything like Gene Autry. He was a warm, friendly, lovable gentleman.

I felt like I was traveling in pretty big company now. From Chillicothe to Kansas City to Texas to a network TV show in Springfield. Little Martin and I had it all. What we still didn't have even by the early 1950s was dressing rooms like they do now. Millie and I at KMBC dressed in school buildings, basements, theaters backstage, in a car or just anywhere we could get. By the fifties at the Jubilee I always dressed at home. But out on the road was still a different story. Nothing fancy like they have today. We didn't do much make-up either. At the Jubilee we all did our own make-up and it wasn't that different from the way we were everyday. There were no makeup people hovering over you like they would do when I did television from California later. Out on the road I wore just about the same as when I was in Kansas City, a little lipstick, a little powder and I was off and running.

It didn't ever take me long to get ready to perform. I still paid attention to my clothes and remembered what Grandma had always told me. "Be modest, because what a person can't see is much more intriguing than what they can see." It was pretty good advice I still remember today. By the end of the first year at the Jubilee I was doing pretty well. I was doing some tours with Red, working a lot with Webb. It was just what I liked to do, stay busy.

On one of those tours with Red we played a stadium somewhere in Texas, I believe. We were all to meet in the room under the stage before show time and when I opened the door by the window there was this guy standing on his head. Naturally Miss Curiosity had to see who it was. So I just went over, looked down at him. It was Pat Boone, Red's son-in-law. He was really popular at that time. I said, "Well I'll be darned. What in the world are you doing standing on your head? He told me with a big smile on his face, if you can smile upside down, he was loosening his vocal cords with exercises and this was one of them. I let him know that I was pleased to be on the same show with him and I'd enjoy talking to him when he got out of that position. He just laughed and said it would take a while. I guess I went on stage and he still was on his head. Seems to me too much blood running up there would make you awfully dizzy. But it didn't seem to bother him.

Biff Collie tells me that I met him in Houston, when we were on that tour but I can't remember him. He was a Number One Disc Jockey and a great supporter of country music. Some years after he and I were married he told me I just didn't have much to say to anyone that night. But then if I didn't really know you I probably wouldn't have. My buddies were all musicians. I'm the musician's best friend. There has always been something special between all of us. I'm a natural born sideman not a star! I've always said that. Biff at this time was married to Floyd Tillman's ex-wife. You remember the song "Slippin' Around":

Seems I always have to slip around
To be with you my dear
Slippin' around, afraid we might be found.
You know I can't forget you
And I've got to have you near.
So I'll just have to slip around,
And live in constant fear.

Well Floyd wrote that for Biff and Marge. I'd probably heard that story and if I was introduced to him. That could be the reason why I didn't say anything to him. I loved Floyd Tillman to pieces. The way he wrote songs was the way I'd like to someday. After that tour I'd be back at the Jubilee and waiting to go on the road again. In the meantime when Webb Pierce came to town he and I always had a ball. We'd go to the movies, especially if there was a Faron Young movie on. He'd laugh till he was almost sick sometimes. Faron was an up and coming country singer, kind of like a younger version of Webb and he'd made it to the movies.

One cowboy movie of Faron Young's had Faron getting off his horse to fight some guy. The next frame had a double about Faron's size rush in tennis shoes and fight the guy off. We laughed so much. I guess we saw that movie about two times and then he told everyone at the Jubilee about it, and probably everyone in Nashville.

Let me tell you, Webb and I were buddies. I said when he came to town we had a ball, like best friends do. We'd go eat, listen to new songs, go to the movies, talk with Lucky Moeller about new bookings, hear all the gossip he knew about Nashville and we became great friends. Chuck Bowers became a part of the group and we did everything. We could have fun!

There was only one thing, well maybe two things that bothered me about Webb. One, he drank quite a bit, and two, was when I was on a show with him he wanted me to keep his money for him until he was through partying. One night I believe it was in Chicago, we did a show he collected his money in cash and handed it to me. I think there was about twenty-five hundred dollars in the package. I didn't count it but that's what he said. He wanted me to give it to him before we left the next day. I tried to get him to put it in the hotel safe, or let Lucky Moeller have you or let anyone else I could think of but he told me he didn't trust anyone but me. I think it was great he trusted me, but I'll tell you I slept with one eye open all night. That was a lot of money for anyone to be earning then. I think I probably made around one-hundred twenty-five dollars and that was tops for a woman. But I had a record contract, I was on a network TV show and traveling in good company so that was a lot of plusses for me.

I mentioned Chuck Bowers always being around Webb and me. He drank too much too, but he was such a likeable guy. He'd give you the shirt off his back if you needed it. Anyway, after the Jubilee one Saturday night, Webb, Chuck and I went out to eat and just mess around for a while. I guess to see what we could get into. Chuck stopped by his house and picked up his little dog. A combination rat terrier and who knows what. We decided to go back to the hotel and play music and listen to Webb's new recordings. By the time we got back there, Chuck was feeling no pain. The night desk clerk gave us a funny look, we were probably noisy and when he spied Chuck's dog. Chuck was carrying him. The desk clerk came out from behind the counter. Chuck had already started upstairs to the mezzanine, I don't know why but he was on the stairs and the desk clerk was after him. The next thing Webb and I knew was the desk clerk was lying on the floor in front of us. Chuck had kicked him down there. Webb was so calm, he asked Chuck, "Why'd you do that fella?" Chuck told him that the clerk called his dog a S.O.B."Ain't nobody gonna call my dog that. You can say anything about my family but you don't call my dog names."

The desk clerk was still lying at our feet and Webb took a roll of bills out of his pocket and gave them to him. He said something like, "Why don't you get up and go back to work and don't call anyone names anymore, till you know who they are."

Webb taught me a lot about listening to music you were going to record. He was really a very smart businessman. He told me if you could listen to a song over and over it was a hit. He should know he had plenty of them. Also, if you could write it, it would even be better. At that time I wasn't writing all that much, but I always remembered what he said. I did owe Webb a great deal. He got me my first recording contract. He used me on all his shows and I'm sure always gave me a good recommendation. Years later when Willie and Webb recorded together I was hoping they'd go on tour and I'd see Webb again so I could thank him for all he did for me. I didn't get the chance to and I didn't get to see him or talk to him before he died. So now I would like very much to say, "Thank you Webb, what a great buddy you were." "I'll never forget you. Much Love always."

I mentioned that Webb and I were in Chicago, during the Jubilee years and I worked a lot with Pee-Wee King there. He had a television show at a theater just down the street from the Planters Hotel where everyone stayed. One time I was dressed up and hurrying to get to the theater and my high heel went down in one of those holes in a manhole cover. I did my part of the show standing on one foot. I felt like a stork. Another highlight I got from working at the Jubilee was getting to work with Leon McAuliffe in Tulsa, Oklahoma. This was a television show and then on down to the big ballroom where he played. Again, I felt like I was back with my Texas friends. I remembered Leon from Bob Wills's days as in, "Take it away Leon" always gave me a thrill. I tried to go there as much as I could without wearing out my welcome. The Little Martin and I were certainly getting around. In doing these shows I was again meeting a lot of people that would always be in my life at one time or another.

During this time I really hadn't thought too much about going on to the Grand Old Opry. Jean Shepherd, Hawkshaw Hawkins, had already gone and usually someone was always talking about going. But when I was in Nashville recording, I did have a chance to meet Jim Denny who booked all the talent for the Opry. He wasn't married at the time to Dolly his secretary, but she and I became such good friends that she almost always let me know what was going on in and around Nashville, when I was there. By this time I had a better offer to record records from Columbia Records. Mr. Don Law the producer for Columbia talked to me and felt they, Columbia, would be better for me. I really hadn't had all that much success on ABC Paramount so I decided it would be right. I was for the next few years to have a great association with Columbia and Don Law. He is responsible for my recording with Lefty Frizzell on "No One to Talk to But the Blues." I just happened to come by the studio and he said, "Lefty needs a harmony singer. Go in there, Shirley."

I just walked in the studio and stood by Lefty and all of a sudden I knew it was going to be easy to sing with him. He had a nice voice, very different, and he was a very easygoing person. We maybe had two cuts on the song and it was perfect. Now in 1992, I heard from Bear Music out of Nashville that there was a CD. I had to send a picture of me thirty years earlier. That wasn't too difficult. I don't have any "today" pictures, but I have a lot of "yesterdays."

Just a little more about Lefty. That same night after the recording at about three or four in the morning, I heard someone kicking at my door. I asked who it was. It was Lefty. I opened the door and he stood there with all the makings for a big party in his arms. When Lefty was drinking he was a little hard to deal with and I had to threaten him that I would call the management if he didn't go away. I'm really sorry that it worked out that way. Actually all he wanted to do was celebrate a hit for Lefty Frizzell and Shirley Caddell.

Back to the Jubilee. Where Gene Autry seemed cold to me in Kansas City, by contrast Smiley Burnette was one of the most warm, wonderful persons I've ever met. I told him I'd spent my money to see him and he said, "Lots of folks have Shirley, or I wouldn't be where I am today." I remember he always stayed after the television part and signed autographs and you could have your picture made with him. I knew him as Frog. And when he'd do that deep voice I just was a little kid again.

Hard to believe I was twenty-two years old, the Little Martin was twelve and I was still in awe of people. We had a cute kid come to the Jubilee when she was only about six or seven years old. I think Red called her "Little Miss Dynamite." If he didn't he should have because she was. She lived up the street from me with her mother, brothers and sisters, and even at such a tender age she knew exactly what she was going to do and she told you too. She could sing the fire out of "Jambalaya" and anything else she did. She'd tell you she was going to be bigger than anyone in the music business and that she was taking care of her family too. She did just what she said she was going to do. Red's Manager Dub Allbritton got a hold of her and she was a rocket to being a star. I saw her several years later in Nashville in Jim Denny's office. He'd taken over her personal appearances. She had come from high school, still had her cheerleading outfit on, and she looked so cute. She showed me a ring that Mr. Denny had made for her, one like he wore on his middle finger, an odd design, kind of like an arrow. She was so proud and who wouldn't be? Mr. Denny was somebody.

That little girl I'm talking about is Ms. Brenda Lee and I knew her when she was just a little girl. Hard to believe I was a little girl like that too with all those dreams and plans. If I had met someone like Red Foley or maybe Dub, maybe I would have already been somebody. But again I was content to be who I was.

The only thing I thought about was if I'd made the money I could have helped my folks more. That would have really made me feel good. I knew Dad was still trucking and by this time they weren't at 1100 Locust anymore. I got to visit them enough to see they were okay. They kept Rusty and adopted him as one of the family. I believe that dog lived till he was about sixteen years old. After I brought him from Texas he lived with them until I took him to California with Biff and me. The Jubilee was getting bigger and bigger. Si Siman tells me it went to the NBC network on January 25, 1954. By this time they have guest stars, Jim Reeves, Sonny James, Webb Pierce, Carl Smith, Tex Ritter, and Rex Allen. They've also added Pete Stamper who did wonderful comedy.

[Carl Smith and me]

I would come by from California at the height of my career and appear with Sonny James. I really hoped that Red Foley would be the host, but he was vacationing at the time. I wanted him to see the lady I'd grown into and how polished I was at being on television. The only time I would see Red Foley again was when Willie and I were living in Fort Worth, Texas. We were on a show with Red, Tammy Wynette, George Jones and several others. He came over to our house and do you know he didn't ask Willie to sing. He wanted to hear "Are You Lonesome For Me Annabelle" one more time. If I had my way I'd hope the angels in heaven were playing that for him right now. What a wonderful man.

Times were changing for me and I was getting ready to do something different. I'd been on the Jubilee for one-and-a-half years and I'd worked on the road with almost anybody and I was in the mood to move. The year was 1954, I was twenty-three, Little Martin was thirteen, and she was all I had to pack. I was going to start looking for something that paid a little more money and not so much hard work. That sounds lazy, doesn't it? But really I wasn't at all lazy.

Because of Dolly Denny, who was married to Jim Denny, I was going to find a rainbow. The rainbow was a touring show, out on the road six weeks, off one week, then back on the road again. Two-hundred fifty dollars a week. Just riding around enjoying the country. Wrong! There's much more to it than this.

What I have to tell you is quite a story. All the events that I'm telling actually happened. I will tell you their names but if they find out I told you, don't say it was me. But before I go on to the Phillip Morris show I would like to thank all the people involved in the Ozark Jubilee. First Si Siman for hiring me, Mr. Fred Raines our floor director and good friend, Mr. Bryan Bisney our director for teaching me a little about television. Red Stattery our wonderful announcer and most of all the entertainers that I've grown to know and love all these years. Some of us are still living, not many of us, but some, and when Si Siman and I talked just recently I heard the sound in his voice, the same as mine, pride in what we did. God Bless you all. God Bless the Ozark Jubilee!

A New Adventure

The year was1954 and not only was I changing but the whole world was changing. I don't recall the exact date I left the Jubilee. Si said he would look it up for me, but I do remember the reason. Dolly Denny suggested to Jim who was looking for a female country singer that he should contact me. He had seen me on the Jubilee and knew my work on stage and with recordings so he called and ask if I'd be interested in joining the show. This show was a traveling show with another girl singer from New York, Mimi Roman, and a country band headed up by Dale Potter, a terrific fiddle player. There was Sammy Pruitt, Johnny Seibert, a comedian, Bun Wilson a quartet, among them Norris Wilson, the great songwriter now and Ronnie Self a sort of rock and roll entertainer who had guested on the Jubilee, and last but not least "Little Jimmy Dickens." Jimmy and I would be taking Goldie Hill and Carl Smith's places while they went on vacation. The MC for the show would be Mr. DJ himself, Biff Collie, from Houston.

Later the show would prove to be so successful that Phillip Morris would keep me and Jimmy Dickens when Goldie and Carl would come back and add some more people and go touring all over the United States. I didn't know at the time and no one bothered to tell me, Phillip Morris was being boycotted through the south for donating money to the NAACP and so they needed to do something to "get good will back," and we were supposed to be the good will. A big show like that could be seen for nothing. At first the people had to show a package of Phillip Morris cigarettes, but later they did away with that.

A few days before I was to leave with the show I drove to Chillicothe picked up my sister Mary, Mom and Grandma and had them go to Nashville with me. They would keep my car and come get me when I had a week off. I would be flying into Kansas City most of the time but once or twice they came to Nashville. My sister was funny on trips over to Nashville. She was so scared of all the bridges we crossed to get there and at each one she'd get down on the floor of the car and cover up. I didn't understand the covering up but if it made her feel better it was all right with me. I didn't really get to be a buddy to my sister. I loved her for sure and my brother too.

The sad part was I wasn't with brother and sister as we grew up. My brother would be killed in a car accident in 1967 and all I could think about his passing was, I wish I had known him better. It seems like our relationship ended when I left for Kansas City and I guess that's true. I saw him over the years and I knew he still played music but that's all I knew. My sister and I would grow closer when I separated from Willie.

When we finally made it to Nashville most everyone was there ready to get going. We all stayed in the James Robertson Hotel and after my folks left, Mr. Jim Denny called and asked me to come up by his office. He needed to talk to me. This talk would lead to him firing me and rehiring me in the same night.

It sure is a funny world. From singing on the sidewalks, to schoolhouses, from war bond drives to political rallies. From radio to Texas night clubs to network television and now to a touring country music show originating in Nashville, Tennessee just a few blocks from the Grand Ole Opry in the Ryman Auditorium. Could it be I'd made it? I sure had come a long way from someone who was twenty-three years old but I still have a long way to go.

I decided that I'd better get up to Jim's office as quick as I could so I rushed up the street to see him. He started talking to me about the road, entertainers and that we needed to do an extra special job for Phillip Morris. I told him I was truly flattered at his hiring me and would do the best job I could for them. Then his talk began leading into a more personal side. He told me since Mimi Roman and I were the only girl singers on the bus. We would be surrounded by men trying to take us out. This would be a big mistake if we let them and all would not be harmonious on the bus. In other words the guys would be at one another's throats and we'd all be fighting.

I assured him that I'd come to Nashville for a job, I wasn't looking for a man and I didn't have any intentions whatsoever of going with anyone on the bus. The talk ended and I went on back to the hotel to eat supper. About the time I sat down Biff Collie, who would be our MC, and Gary Pike, who was the advance man for Phillip Morris, joined me for supper. We were laughing and talking, introducing ourselves, getting to know one another and I'm finding out what the show is all about. I have to tell you Gary, as I said was an advance man, he would go ahead of the bus, make our reservations at the hotel, see when we played that night and try to establish some good relationships with the radio and TV for us. Also, he was and this is so funny allergic to tobacco. Later when we were in the tobacco warehouses in Winston Salem, NC. His eyes would be so red and weeping, what a terrible situation to be in with an allergy and working for a tobacco company. But he did it anyway.

Mr. Denny and Dolly came in to the restaurant and when he saw me, Biff and Gary having such a wonderful evening, he got really upset. He came over to the table and said to me, "Didn't I just talk to you about all this?" I was really surprised and at first thought he was kidding but then I could see he wasn't. He, Mr. Denny, was drinking a little bit and he didn't see things the way they were. He said something else, I said something else, and before you knew it, I said why don't you take your job, Mr. Denny, I'm going home and that's exactly what I intended to do. I walked out, and Biff and Gary walked out, too. They tried to calm me down but I was determined to go home. I went up to my room and Dolly Denny followed me. She's such a sweet, sweet person. She tried to talk to me, told me Jim had had a few drinks and didn't mean what he'd said. I think I might have been crying. I do when I'm mad sometimes and as fast as I was putting my things into the suitcase, she was taking them out.

Someone knocked on the door. It was Gary and Biff and Don Law, my record producer, and they all crowded into the little room that I had. Picture this: They're trying to talk to me, I'm mad, Dolly's trying to talk to me, I'm packing, they're unpacking, Don's trying to tell me to think things over, don't be so hasty. I've got the Little Martin and I'm leaving. Suddenly someone knocks on the door. By this time the rooms crowded anyway so they just walked in. It's Jim. He told me how sorry he was, he didn't mean what he'd said, and he apologized. I guess I told him don't ever say anything like that to me again. I was a lady and I'd always do the right thing when it came to my work. Famous last words: Within a year or so, Biff and I would be married. Don't fool with anyone on the bus, indeed!

Everything was patched up then and I finally got everyone out of my room so I could get some rest before we left the next morning. About four the next morning my phone rang. It was Jim. He said, "I really only wanted to see if your still here."

"You have a terrible temper, don't you?" he said. I knew I did. So I told him, "Just please go to sleep," I'd be on the bus when it got ready to leave. So that's how you get hired, fired and rehired in the space of a few hours. I believe it was a first. No one over the years has been able to repeat what happened to me.

The next morning everyone on the bus was ready for me. We had, I didn't know at the time, a bunch of practical jokers and everyone framed up this story. Dale Potter asked me if I knew that when we would cross a state line I would have to get out of the bus and walk. I looked at him like one of us is crazy but he continued on with the story they'd made up. Well, naive person that I was, I thought he was telling me the truth, since everyone else agreed with him. I just told him to tell me whenever he wanted me to walk. I thought this is nuts, but it must be true. I asked him if Mimi had to get off too and he told me no, she had already done her walks. I wondered if I was back at KMBC again with all the jokes they played on me, but I went along with it. They told me later they were testing me as far as going along with a joke. When I found out that none of what he said was true I laughed along with them.

A nutty bunch of folks they were, but we were all going to be friends for the next six weeks or more so I didn't make waves. And friends we were. For a touring road show we didn't ever have much trouble between us. Mimi and Johnny Seibert, Carl Smith's Steel Player, had already decided to be together, though they acted like nobody knew it. They'd get separate rooms with a door in between. Oh well if they wanted it that way we didn't care.

Me, I was one of the guys. My seat was in the back of the bus. The long seat, where I could see out the back, when I wasn't sleeping. It was the seat everyone gathered if you wanted to sing and we did, and where everyone visited and we had time to do that too.

Our first job was in Tallahassee, Florida and we were in the middle of a football field. It seemed to me we were pretty important. We were riding around in a big scenic cruiser with everyone's name on the side. That was really impressive for those days. I would do three songs, and then another part of a song at the end where we had our final stage appearance. I was on second. Later they'd move me to next to closing just before Jimmy Dickens and we'd pick the show back up for the finale. I don't mind saying we had one of the best shows out of Nashville: Red Sovine, George Morgan, Little Jimmy Dickens, Mimi, Biff, the band, the quartet, Ronnie Self and guest stars galore later.

I remember eating ice cream in a restaurant in Tallahassee, Florida before the show and "Little Jim" came in. He was telling me how bad his bursitis was and that he could hardly turn his head. He thought he'd have to quit before long. I know I sympathized with him and said I hoped he could finish this tour. That was almost forty years ago and Jimmy is going on stronger than ever. He'll never quit. Entertainment is in his blood.

From Tallahassee to completely on down and around the coast of Florida the Phillip Morris Show traveled with story after story to be told and that was only to be the first 6 weeks. The show would continue to live after Biff and I left. We'd been on it for one and one-half years and most of a lifetime. When you're with people night and day in a small space as we were on the bus you get to know almost everything about everyone—their moods, likes and dislikes, what foods everyone eats, and what kind of music we each liked.

Speaking of music, Sammy Pruitt our lead guitar man had the greatest collection of Django Reinhart records I've ever heard in my life. Django was one of the most wonderful guitar players I've ever heard and he didn't have fingers on his hand. Some way I'm not sure how whether by accident or birth he only had stubs for fingers. I'm talking jazz guitar not country. But he could play anything. I'll have to ask Harold Bradley, now President of Local 257, American Federation of Musicians in Nashville, the most recorded guitarist in the world, just what was wrong with his hands. I'm sure he'll know.

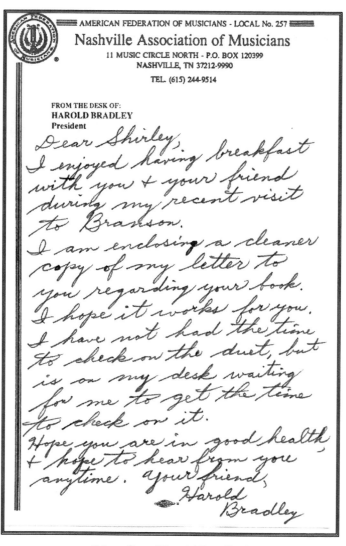

[Note from Harold Bradley]

Anyway when we had a day off, which was usually Sunday, we'd all party Saturday night after our show into the next day or the wee hours of the morning and you can bet you'd hear Django Reinhart records. How Sammy managed to carry all those 33 1/3 RPM albums on the bus I'll never know, but he did. Sammy and I had met before in the years I was at KMBC. He would be on the road with a band, I think Hank Williams band, for a while he always tried to date me. The date never happened, neither one of us understood why but it didn't. But he would be one of my musician friends with me forever. I had an occasion to talk to his sister-in-law Jeanne Pruitt, a wonderful songwriter and singer and she told me Sammy had passed on. I remember all the good times Sammy, I love you.

Anyway on those days off we gave everyone who was our neighbors if we were in a motel, or if in a hotel, the management, a bad time. Not that we were doing anything wrong. We'd be relaxing and playing music, too loud I know, and singing and laughing. We did a lot of laughing. Mimi and Johnny considered us the "Wild Bunch." Gary Pike got so he'd join us and when little Johnny Roventini was with us, he did too. You know, he was the "Call for Phillip Morris" Johnny. I asked him if the story I'd heard about his getting a job with Phillip Morris was true. I'd heard that he was a bellboy in an Atlanta Hotel and a long time ago before there were intercoms and all that stuff he'd go through the lobby and call out the person's name if they had a call. Someone from the company had him do Phillip Morris and when he did "Call for Phillip Morris" everybody just flipped out. He had the sweetest voice and he was so tiny, smaller than Little Jim. Both of them together were quite a pain.

Once when the KKK was following us because Phillip Morris had given a big donation to the NAACP, as I mentioned, Dale Potter banged on something that sounded like a gun. When it popped, Johnny dove down between the seats because things were really tense and he was scared. Little Jimmy Dickens came back and took the pillowcase off my pillow and put it on. He went up the aisle and told everyone he was too small to fight, he'd just join them.

I must tell you that the KKK people did follow us and sit along the road, and we weren't allowed to stay in some towns in the south. This was the reason for the good will show: we were to promote Phillip Morris without promoting. No big fuss, just good will. But some southerners don't forget anything. As we got deeper and deeper into the south, things did get worse. It wasn't too bad in Florida, but when we got over to the Carolinas and Georgia and the Deep South, things were bad. Sometimes we had federal escorts, other times we'd drive the bus right into the building up to the stage, do the show, and take on off for the next town because they wouldn't let us stay in the motels.

Our paychecks would be mailed to us and many times we wouldn't be able to get them cashed. We'd have to wait until arrangements could be made in another town. By now everyone has explained to me why I was riding through the country, taking a chance on being blown up and liking it. Isn't that crazy, but I did it and I wasn't ever too scared. Once in a while I was somewhat apprehensive but never scared.

All of us on the bus usually stayed pretty close to each other in case someone needed help of any kind. Speaking of help, one night, I believe it was in Mississippi; the guys all got together and went out on the town. I heard they all got really drunk, all except for the one who told me. Even the road manager went along, and the next day our drummer showed up at the show with two broken arms, and do you know he played the show in casts that night. I can still see him. I don't know how, but he did. I don't know where they went but all of them looked like they'd been fighting a bunch of cats. I have to laugh now. Maybe I laughed then, I probably did!

They had a rule on the bus: if you weren't there when it got ready to leave, it left without you. So if you overslept or were out too late the night before, you could get in trouble. I think our road manager set that up. Several times different people missed the bus and they'd have to take a taxi or get a car to the next job. After you'd done it once you didn't do it again.

Me, I'm always up at 6:02 A.M. even if I go to bed at 5:00 A.M. Sometimes on the road people hated me 'cause I was always looking for someone to go to breakfast with. Getting up early is a habit, I guess, or it could go along with about the time I was born. The doctor says no one really understands it. But night owls definitely don't like early risers. I was always up, packed and on the bus, ready to get going. I think all the time I was on the road show I only missed performing one or two times. That was because I had a tooth pulled in Ohio, and the dentist up there left some bone chips in my mouth, so by the time we got to Louisiana I had to have oral surgery. And people think we had it easy, moving from state to state. Believe me it wasn't easy, and it still isn't. Maybe it's a little easier today. But truly there is no place like home.

Today most hotels have laundry facilities available to you. A washer and dryer would have truly been a blessing then. We would get to our room and I would spend my time washing and wringing dry the things I needed. Several of the guys told me they did the same thing. Remember this was six weeks on the road. You've got to figure out how to spend your money, do what little you do extra, like eating and entertainment and always someone goes broke and needs a little help. That's happened to me too, especially when I had my bad tooth problem. But everyone in the bus family was always eager to lend a hand. Like I said, we always pretty well looked out for one another.

Two of the kindest men I've ever met who were on the show were Red Sovine and George Morgan. Two of the greatest practical jokers I've ever met, were on the show too, Red Sovine and George Morgan. Their jokes got so bad on all of us that we banded together and made them drive behind the bus in their own car. Red would drive for six weeks and then George would drive. I'd look out the back window and see if they were up to anything or I should say up to no good, and report back to everyone else.

One of the jokes I'll never forget happened down in Florida. Red built a little fire of twigs outside George's door at the motel where we were staying. Then he got down on his hands and knees and blew the smoke into the room. He had all of us alerted as to what he was happening, then after the smoke was going good, he started yelling, "Fire! Fire!" and suddenly the door opened and out jumped George in his underwear, running like the dickens. Everyone laughed and as usual after the initial shock, George laughed too. I'm sure he got Red back again with some joke or another but when he did get him back Red didn't say anything.

The one thing I haven't mentioned in all the years of traveling around is fans. As long as there are fans there will be entertainers. I don't always like to say fans, I'd rather say friends, 'cause that's what they are. They are loyal, kind, loving people who will follow you to the end of the earth. They bring you food, gifts, birthday presents, Christmas presents, send cards, call radio stations and do all those many things to boost your ego sky high. I'm still meeting people who were fans of mine way back on KMBC in Kansas City, and the other night I met a fella who said his dad always listened to me when he was doing his chores on the farm. Isn't that great?

Well the Phillip Morris show had lots of fans even if we were in dangerous territory. George, Red and Little Jim probably had more than anyone. When Carl Smith came back to the show, I'd say he did too because he had several Number 1 hit records out. Goldie Hill, who would later marry Carl, and who was my airport buddy, had a wonderful following too. She was and still is such a beautiful woman. Argolda Hill, she told me was her name, and she was from, Texas. She had some of the most beautiful western costumes that she wore on the show. One I really remember was a gold western dress. I believe she said "Nudie" the tailor to the stars had made it for her. I met Nudie a few years later when I was on TV in California and he made me a beautiful dress for a rodeo where I was performing. I really felt like someone after I wore it.

Before we were married, Biff had fans, or should I say girlfriends in almost every town. I guess I liked him from the start. He was a very handsome man. Black hair, dark eyes, good build and that's what I like. Black hair and dark eyes get me every time. Maybe because I have such a fair complexion, with red hair and light skin. Anyway he had girls falling all over him. We'd start pulling into town and he'd send me to the front of the bus so he could change clothes and meet someone after the show. He was a very busy fellow. I got a look at a couple of the girls he had, one wasn't too bad but the other, I'd rather not say. But everyone has different tastes, don't they? Sometimes he'd get back on the bus and would tell some wild stories. We were his family, so why shouldn't he tell us what happened.

We were one big family, rolling along, with Gary Pike, our advance man, forging the trail for us up ahead in his MG or whatever that little car he drove was. I felt like we were trailblazers, or pioneers.

Now as far as what today they call groupies, we had those too! In fact about the second time we were out for another six weeks, we had girls who followed the bus for several weeks into West Virginia, all up and down the roads. The guys would have me look out the back and see if they were still behind us and there the three of them would be in this green car. One girl, I can see them now, was as big as a Mack Truck, the other two just regular size and not bad looking. I didn't talk to them much. They were just following along for the men. I didn't really understand all that then and even today I don't understand it. Whatever turns you on.

Anyway all of us on the bus decided we'd play a terrible joke on Gary Pike, the next time we stopped overnight. This is really bad. We would tell the "Mack Truck" that Gary had fallen for her but he was bashful and didn't know how to ask her up to his room. I imagine it was Red who set the scene. He'd get an extra key and after Gary went to bed, he'd unlock the door for her and she could be with Gary, and he could tell her how much he cared for her. The night presented itself, Gary got drunker than a skunk and someone helped him to his room and made sure he was asleep. Then they let "Old Mack" in and we'd just let nature take its course.

The next morning all of us, including the bus driver waited in the restaurant. It seems there wasn't an elevator in this hotel so you could see directly up the stairs, waiting for Gary to come downstairs. He did, about half-dressed and screaming like a panther, "Where are you people?" Naturally the guys ran to meet him. He was hysterical. They asked him what happened. By this time they had him in the restaurant and sat him down. He said, "I turned over in bed and this baby walrus said, 'Kiss me good morning' and I started screaming and ran out of the room." He didn't give the poor girl a chance.

But after that we didn't see them or their car anymore. So much for groupies. I never did tell Gary what happened and I don't think anyone else did. All of us were deeply concerned this had to happen to him. The Wild Bunch had struck again.

I had become, after we'd been out about the second or third time, "Ms. Mom" on the bus. I had a huge purse I carried that had practically everything you'd need to survive on the road except food. Aspirins, needles and thread—someone was always tearing something—Band-Aids, extra toothbrushes, safety pins. There wasn't anything you could name that I didn't have in that bag.

Also, because Grandma had instilled in me a familiarity with home remedies and homespun advice years ago, I could give my opinion on what was wrong if anyone was sick. One night Norro Wilson came up to me before the show and told me he didn't feel well. I put my hand on his forehead and it was hot. I told him I believed he had a temperature, which he did. Then I said, "Let me see inside your mouth." I told him "Kiddo, you've got the measles," and he was petrified. I didn't see anything to get alarmed about. You had them for three days and it was over.

What was funny was he was part of a quartet and by the end of three days the whole group had the measles. They all went ahead and worked. I knew they were sick, and I watched as the spotlight picked up their faces and they had put make-up on to hide the little red spots. They asked me not to tell. They were afraid they would have to go back to Tennessee. I didn't think they would, but I didn't tell.

From time to time Mr. Denny and some of the executives from the Phillip Morris Company would come out on the bus for a few days and see how the show was progressing. That's when we all would straighten up and tried to be good. It was hard but we tried. I was still not making any waves, so Mr. Denny was extremely happy. He didn't even say anything at all about our talk in the hotel before when I first left with the show and I didn't ever mention it again. Things like that are best left alone. He seemed extremely happy that the show was being accepted so much. I believe that Phillip Morris hadn't expected so much acceptance or success with us. But when they saw what was happening, they all decided to make it a goodwill show all over the United States.

The plan was Carl and Goldie would return, Jimmy and I would stay without a break, and we'd go everywhere. From time to time we'd have guest stars go with us all over the country. One I remember vividly was Patsy Cline. She was with us two or three days and what a terrific entertainer she was. The one thing I remember was she was about seven or eight months pregnant and she was wearing a waist cincher. Well I wore one too, but I wasn't pregnant. These cinchers made you have a very tiny waist if that's what you wanted. Well hers had strings like Grandma's corset and she asked me to help her put it on. I told her, "Patsy this thing is way too tight."

She said, as only Patsy could, "Hell, pull the damn thing tighter, Shirley. It will make me sing in a higher key." When I saw her later in Las Vegas I asked her if she remembered that and she said, "How could anyone forget almost not being able to sing?" Then she laughed, the Patsy laugh I liked. The last time I saw her would have been in Nashville, just after Willie left Ray Price, and we were taking off to Reno to get me a divorce. She wished us good luck in everything we tried. She was a great lady with a big beautiful heart. She was also super tough for a girl singer in knowing what she wanted and doing it her way.

Love on the Road

I don't exactly know how Biff and I began to be together so much. It seemed on Sundays we always managed to eat together, go find a band someplace and listen to them and just maybe way down deep I probably wanted him to really like me. I think the turning point might have been in New Orleans. This was right after I had my oral surgery and I still wasn't feeling all that great. Biff and I caught a ride with someone from Biloxi, Mississippi to New Orleans, then he was going to take a plane to San Antonio to his parents, and I'd be going to Kansas City, Missouri, where mine would pick me up at the airport then go on to Chillicothe. I was really sick, my mouth hurt so bad I couldn't eat. He took me to the Absinthe House on Bourbon St. and he left a card with our names on it just like everyone else had. What a wonderful place to see New Orleans. I think it was so much different than any other place I'd ever been, and I loved it.

Maybe the setting was romantic? I don't think so. I'm not sure you can be romantic when you're in pain. Anyhow, we just got one hotel room to rest in. He was leaving after me, so we'd only have a few hours. I think we told each other that we really cared for each other and, remember now; we had been out on the road for quite a while. If you can be with someone for twenty-four hours a day and still like that person when the day is over, that's a pretty good test, I think. We knew what the other liked and all that kind of little talk we hadn't been able to do on the bus.

Biff had been married before, I'd been married before and we didn't want to make any more mistakes. Anyway we parted and after I had gotten to Chillicothe, he called me to see if I made it all right and he told me he'd be glad when we got back together again. We'd just gotten home and we were eager to get back out on the road again. Needless to say, Little Martin was just as anxious as we were to get back with the Wild Bunch. She'd always do some nightly melodies in the back of the bus, with the quartet and Jimmy. "I'll meet you in the morning" was one of our favorites to sing. It was an old gospel song that Bill Monroe did.

I'll meet you in the morning by the bright riverside,
When all sorrow has drifted away
I'll be standin' at the portals when the gates open wide
At the close of life's long weary day

I'll meet you in the morning with a how do you do
And we'll sit down by the river and when all the rapture is renewed
You'll know me in the morning by the smile that I wear
When I meet you in the morning In the city that is built four square

I will meet you in the morning in the sweet by and by
And exchange the old cross for a crown
There will be no disappointments and nobody shall die
In that land when life's sun goeth down

When it was time to go back out, I think I probably met the bus somewhere. It was much easier than having Mom drive all the way to Nashville. Biff met me at the bus and gave me a beautiful watch and his words to me were, "Let's consider this an engagement present." Was I ever happy. I got on the phone and called home to tell everyone as quick as I could. I'm gonna have a home one of these days! Everyone on the bus was congratulating us and wishing us well and wondering when we got serious. We probably were wondering that ourselves. Things didn't change that much, we still went on playing jokes and being ourselves like always. After all I'm only engaged. One thing did change a little, Biff was very good friends with Carl Smith. Carl drove his car, and Goldie rode with him, so quite a few times we rode in his car. You know I did miss the bus, but I didn't say anything. I still wished for a sink of dirty dishes and a home and family and I thought I had found someone very special in Biff.

103

The road manager we had at this time was something of a character himself—Charlie. At one time he did security for Hank Williams. His job, he told us, was to keep Hank sober, if that was possible. One story he told us was that they were in an auditorium somewhere and he put Hank on the second floor of the building in a small room with only a tiny window. There was no way Hank was gonna get drunk before the show. When he went to get him at showtime he unlocked the door and Hank was so drunk he couldn't even stand. He had managed somehow to get the window open and had kept hollering until someone noticed him. Hank had torn his T-shirt and underwear into strips and forced them out the window and people below had tied a big old whiskey bottle on the strips. That's unbelievable, but true.

I had the pleasure of sitting with Jim Stafford and Buck Trent a few nights back, and Jim told a story about Hank being drunk and not being able to perform. So they just propped him up on the corner of the stage and the band played all his music. The audience went wild. At least even if he didn't sing he showed up for the show.

Remember I told you about fans, faithful until the end, and even after the end? Well, it seems the fans I had and the fans Biff had were delighted that we were engaged. Even Jim Denny was delighted. Maybe even Phillip Morris too.

We'd found love on the road. As I look back now I'm wondering if what Biff and I felt at that time was just infatuation. We didn't say love. As I said, when you're together for twenty-four hours a day something is bound to happen. Anyway it did and in some little town in the north we were married, with Carl Smith as best man and Goldie as my maid of honor. It wasn't a big ceremony, just very private. None of the bus family knew it until it was over, and I was Mrs. Hiram Abiff Collie. We honeymooned that night after the show on peaches and cookies. Every year on our anniversary we had the same menu.

The next day we'd be leaving again. Biff was going to take me on the next break to San Antonio, Texas, to meet his family. My family had already met Biff when we played St. Joseph, Missouri and they really liked him. So you can believe I was a little bit nervous. But after meeting everyone in Texas they treated me so nice, and if I remember right, they had a big picnic to introduce me to everyone. That's Texas for you. So neighborly.

They understood we wouldn't be staying long, and within a week we were back on the road. This time out Mr. Denny had offered Biff a job as road manager. Charlie had left us, and he took it. This meant more money, not better hours, and since we both were making good money we were doing all right. Biff was always saving some money, which is great if you can do it. He didn't tell me but he had in mind we'd be leaving the show and we'd try to settle somewhere. He thought that Los Angeles, California or New York would be good, I found out later. But until we did that we'd just stay on the show.

Maybe being on the road was better now. I had a husband who thought I was very talented, which was a new experience for me. He was interested in how I presented myself on the show, how I dressed, how I looked—he always wanted me to look my very best. We didn't go around being sloppy on the bus, because you'd get to town and you'd have to go do interviews at the local radio station and promote the show with as many people as possible.

We had gone completely through the southern states and I think we were more than a success. Now we were heading into other territory and being just as successful. I'm not going to be able to list everyone who guested on the Phillip Morris Show because the list is way too long. But anyone who was anyone appeared on that show during the years it played.

Now, instead of washing in the bathtub for one I washed for two. But I didn't mind one bit. In fact I was really happy. I had a good-looking, hard working husband and I was singing and doing what I liked to do. Before my part of the show went on I'd sit offstage and knit, which was one of my favorite hobbies. A girl at the radio station in Kansas City had taught me how. She started me on socks with all different colors. Argyle socks, they're called. But now I was either knitting an afghan or knitting shoes for everyone. In fact, several of my entertainer friends still can picture me sitting behind stage knitting. That's how they remember me.

Just recently I saw Johnny Russell a very talented and wonderful entertainer, of the Grand Ole Opry, and the "Act Naturally" fame. He said, "Do you remember the last time I saw you?" I couldn't place when, but he knew it was at the Opry and I was backstage waiting for Willie to perform. I was knitting. He, Johnny, stopped to say hello and asked me what I was knitting. I said, "A cover for Ernest Tubbs Bus" and then I said, as he recalled, "I'm practicing on knitting a sweater for you." We surely had a good laugh together.

Biff did a part in the show where he played the trumpet and then at the end of his song he'd do a somersault off the stage. He always landed right side up. There were a few times I didn't know if he would make it or not but he never failed.

My spot in the show had been changed from the first part to next to the closing. They tell me that's a difficult spot to have. Your audience is tired and with Red Sovine, who was on in the middle with his recitations, George Morgan with his ballads following him, they told me, "We've slowed the show down to a crawl." Being on then was really quite nice. The Little Martin and I would go out and liven things up. My last song was a yodeling song. I'd either do "He Taught me to Yodel" or "I Betcha my Heart I Love You." Carl had a record of "I Betcha my Heart" and sometimes he closed with that song. In fact on his radio show he did. I believe it could have been his theme song.

Speaking of radio shows, country at this particular time was picking up some, and we were getting more country music stations. Of course it wasn't like now, with 3,000-plus stations nationwide, but country was on the move. I did a little investigating and when I was on the Brush Creek Follies in the late forties it, the Follies was ranked the number two radio show in the nation. Number one was the WLS Chicago Barn dance, then the Brush Creek Follies, then the Grand Ole Opry, followed by the Louisiana Hayride. The Hayride would bring us some wonderful entertainers, like Hank Williams, Jim Reeves, Faron Young, and on and on. The Chicago Barn dance had Red Foley, Peewee King, Eddy Arnold, George Gobel—yes I said George Gobel, with his big guitar—Lulabelle and Scotty, I always loved them in the movies with Roy Acuff. We would get great entertainers from everywhere.

The Brush Creek Follies had run for twenty-eight years. I'm not sure how long the WLS Barn dance went and we all know the Grand Ole Opry will possibly run forever. As long as someone sings, plays a guitar, a mouth harp, fiddle or whatever, somebody will put them on the radio. Always in the car when we traveled from the Jubilee, I'd have to have the radio on WSM so I could hear the Friday and Saturday night Opry.

Radio has always been to me the most wonderful invention in the world since white bread. The days of live entertainment are about gone. Everything these days is on television. If you are lucky, you'll be able to hear some great DJs across this country. Without them, entertainers would be nothing. Biff Collie was one of those tremendous DJs. After we left the road show he would go on to be one of the best in California and later he entered the DJ Hall of Fame. He always has been a very influential person in radio and country music, and that he believed in my abilities made me very proud.

One day after we'd been out again for another six weeks, Biff asked me where I'd like to live, Los Angeles, California or New York. We had been to New York with the show and I didn't care too much about living there, so naturally I said California. He told me the radio market for him was good in either place and he said he thought California might be better. He had an aunt who lived in San Gabriel and we could go and look things over. I was hearing that we were going to be leaving Phillip Morris. I didn't know when, but I understood he would be giving them notice and we wouldn't be out the next time.

SINGER SHIRLEY CADDELL WITH PHILIP MORRIS SHOW

Redheaded Shirley Caddell, a Chillicothe girl, will be one of the singing attractions when the touring "Philip Morris Country Music Show" plays St. Louis at the Keil Auditorium next Monday night.

A Columbia recording artist, Shirley, until she joined the all-star country music show, was a regular cast member of the nationally-televised "Ozark Jubilee." Earlier, she was a star of the "Millie and Sue" team over KMBC in Kansas City. She is the daughter of Mr. and Mrs. Henry Simpson of 1305 Calhoun street, Chillicothe.

Recently, Shirley became the bride of Biff Collie, show emcee and radio host of the CBS radio program, the Philip Morris Country Music Show, heard on Sunday nights.

The country music entertainers have been on tour since Jan. 6 of last year, playing six days out of seven. They will play engagements in Belleville, Ill.; Jefferson City, Mo.; Springfield, Mo., and in Kansas at Chanute and Lawrence on the present tour.

1958

We would go to Chillicothe to see my folks, then to San Antonio to see his folks, then on to California. We rode the train from Chicago to Chillicothe and I hated every minute of it. The last show we played was in Chicago. We had a wild kid come on as our guest, in his early twenties, all dressed in white, and could he ever play piano. He even played with his feet, and he turned the piano stool over and I don't know what else. The people went wild. His name, Jerry Lee Lewis, "the Killer." Only he wasn't the Killer then, just some kid from Memphis trying to make it in show business. His performance floored everyone, and Biff and I were still talking about him on the way to Chillicothe. I believe Biff had some insight about the road show, that possibly it wouldn't be running too much longer, so like I said, we told everybody goodbye and got on the train. It was truly like losing a family. They'd been my family for almost two years and the bus had been my home.

And besides, who was going to doctor everybody? No one else carried a big purse like mine full of everything and anything. It was really sad. But I had a new husband and our future lay somewhere away from the Phillip Morris Country Music Show. So away we went to a new adventure. Biff and me and Little Martin. She, the Little Martin, rode the train and hated it too. Probably went all out of tune, but I don't know. I was twenty-four years old, Biff was nine years older than me, and Little Martin was fourteen. She, the Little Martin, was in wonderful shape and I was looking pretty good myself.

I must credit Biff with getting me to really take care of myself. Up to this time, I took things easy, a little make-up, some skirts and blouses and I was ready to go on and perform. But when we got to California, I was going to find things a lot different. From downtown to uptown might be a way to describe it. I think, and this is my own opinion, that California is way ahead of the rest of the world. Someone told me they didn't believe Hollywood was real, that the prop people from the studios would come along Hollywood Boulevard some night and fold all the sets up and leave. After you've been there a while you kind of feel that way too. But at this time in my life I was just happy to be going there.

When we got to Chillicothe we were going to pick up some of my things I'd left with my folks. They didn't want me to take Rusty, my peke, so I didn't, but I'd get him later. I had to go to the dentist in Chillicothe while we were there. I really always made an appointment for one thing or the other when we were on break, so while I was at the dentist office Biff hung around with my dad. I got through at the dentist and called for them to come get me. When I went out the door Biff was standing there and I said, "Where's the car?" He pointed across the street at a two-tone, brown-and-white Chevrolet car. He said, "It's ours. I just bought it." My dad was a great friend and customer of the Chevrolet people in Chillicothe, so I'm sure he took Biff out there. I guess I didn't realize we had that kind of money to pay for a car, but we did.

Biff rented a small U-Haul trailer and in a few days we headed to San Antonio, Texas, to tell his mom and dad goodbye. Everyone acted like we were going to drop off into the ocean when we got there, like we were never coming back. I realized it was the farthest away from my folks that I'd ever been, at least to live. But don't they say, "Love is blind. " By this time I was thinking I was really in love and looking for a place to settle down.

For me and Little Martin we wouldn't stay settled long, and Little Martin's life was really about to move 'cause in a few months she'd be on ABC-TV in Hollywood. But at this particular time, television wasn't really in my mind. I was only thinking of a new adventure for both of us.

It's always been easy for me to move around. People tell me I can adapt to conditions and I guess that's true. Probably, as I look back, I would have been just as happy in San Antonio. What a wonderful place. This time before we left we had to make the tour of the Alamo, and do all those things tourists do. Mostly I just liked to eat all the different kinds of food, and what wonderful Mexican food San Antonio has. Biff's mom and dad showed me all the sights. Before we left, Biff had to call Leon Payne, the wonderful blind songwriter who wrote such hits as "I Love You Because," and many more. He congratulated us on our marriage.

In a few days we packed up Biff's things in the U-Haul and finally got on the road to California. We were somewhere out in the desert when I asked Biff if we could stop so I could get a closer look at the cactus. So since this was partly a leisure trip he did and we both went off looking around just like we were normal folks. All of a sudden we heard this horn blowing and when we looked up we saw the Phillip Morris bus with all our friends and they were stopping. Miles away from anyone, we had a reunion with our family. It was great! We were all hugging and laughing like we hadn't seen each other in years instead of just a few weeks. But that's the way all entertainers are—always together no matter where or how long we're apart we're really always together. It's wonderful!

<u>The Family</u>
It's so good to have the family back together
We have been apart for much too long
It's so good to have the family back together
All of us together here at home.
Each of us have grown up and have families of our own
But we never can forget our happy days at home
Mom and Dad grow older
Toward the twilight of their days
But all of us would travel far
To hear our Mommy say:
It's so good to have the family back together
We have been apart for much too long
It's so good to have the family back together.
All of us together here at home.

The rest of the trip to California seemed uneventful compared to the reunion in the desert, but it was nice to see the country from a car and not from the window of a bus. We went on out to San Gabriel, California to stay with Biff's Aunt Mary until we could get our belongings as to where we were. Of course we decided we had to have a place to live first, but where? We finally set on Hollywood for a while and we got an apartment on Grant Avenue just up the street from the famous Hollywood Boulevard.

It's really funny about the apartment because when we looked for our landlord we met a character actor who did the rentals. When we opened the door I was looking in the face of a movie actor I knew. His name was Charlie Tannen and I'd seen him in dozens of films. He was flattered about my recognizing him and maybe that's why we got the apartment. He told me very few bit players are ever recognized. But remember, I'm a sideman, so I always look at the extra people.

Charlie told me, "Every time you see me in a movie, I'm there for a reason." He was a recovered alcoholic and he was in the picture to keep the star from getting drunk and causing everything to go off schedule. Small world, isn't it? I used to stay up late at night for all-night movies just to watch for him. He was really a nice guy and a super landlord.

We turned in our U-Haul and started to get adjusted to California living. What a difference! Everything was open twenty-four hours, and there were wonderful grocery stores and shops. It was a great place to live.

[Me in California]

Biff opened a bank account and I was beginning to feel we were going to be just another California couple. Biff began making applications at the radio stations, enrolled in the Actor's Studio, and went looking for television commercials. We knew we had to do something before our money ran out. We'd been there a few months, and I hadn't been feeling all that great. I just thought it was because I was off the road and just beginning to relax, but I was too tired.

We found a doctor, Dr. Agar, in Beverly Hills. He was also Liz Taylor's doctor. When we went for our appointment, the doctor said I needed to go to the hospital right away. It turned out I had a cyst in the fallopian tube and I was operated on in the same afternoon. I came through the operation just fine but we found out that I probably wouldn't be able to have children. Biff and I were saddened, because for once in my life I felt like I really wanted to have a family. My ideas of home and family were just the same as when I was riding in the bus wishing I had a sink full of dirty dishes. I had always wished for a huge house, lots of kids, family dinners, birthday and Christmas parties and all the good things I thought that a family had. But it seemed God had other plans for me.

"Country America"

During my recuperation time I began to watch television and a show called "Country America." Biff still didn't have a steady job but he began to do some commercials and he had an interview at the pop station KLAC in Hollywood. My thoughts were with "Country America." How was I going to manage that I didn't know, but I knew I was going to work on that show.

The MC of the show turned out to be a friend of Biff's from Texas, Joe Allison. Joe and Audrey had just written, "He'll Have to Go" for Jim Reeves, so they were really up there in the music business. Biff called him and told him that we were living in Hollywood and needing to work, if there were any openings. Lo and behold, one of the girls on the show was pregnant and would be leaving the soon! She just happened to be a yodeler and a country music singer. What a break—they needed me!

About this time I was doing fine from my operation and I needed to go to ABC-TV for an audition. You know, I didn't have any doubts about getting the job. Seems strange, doesn't it, but it's just like when I auditioned in Kansas City. Everything felt right, and it was. I got the job. As soon as she left I would go to work, just two weeks before Biff was to begin work on KLAC.

We really didn't like living in downtown Hollywood too much. Aunt Mary had a little house behind her big house, and she said if we'd fix it up we were welcome to live there. So we packed up and moved out to San Gabriel, where we could see mountains and flowers and trees and grass. Not that Hollywood doesn't have those things, but it just didn't seem much like home.

Some things we did miss about Hollywood were a little church we went to, singing at the famous Hollywood Canteen on Sundays and the Hollywood Christian Group. The Hollywood Christian Group was a fellowship of entertainers, actors and anyone in show business. It was at a meeting of this group that I met Roy Rogers and, of course, Dale Evans. To be able to associate with people like them was wonderful.

The one thing that shocked me was how small Roy was. He was not very tall and definitely thin. In the movies everything is bigger than life. I can remember getting to see him in the movies at the Grand Theater in Chillicothe. I always thought he was terrific and in real life he was, so warm and friendly. Of course Dale did all the talking but that didn't matter. In this world of entertainers it's awfully nice to have a group like the Hollywood Christian Group.

Everybody knows about the freeways in California, and since we moved to San Gabriel that meant I was going to have to drive into Hollywood to the television studio. Up to this time I was never behind the wheel out there. I just simply wouldn't drive. The freeways were four or five lanes of solid traffic and everyone was going like crazy. But Biff told me this was one thing I had to do, so coming back from Long Beach one day; he stopped and told me to move over to the driver's side. I did, scared to pieces, and headed for home.

I was over in the fast lane and suddenly I heard this beeping behind me. I looked in the mirror. It was a patrolman. I looked at the speedometer. I was going 70 miles per hour! I looked up again and the patrolman signaled for me to pull over. He drove up by my window. I remember I was white as a sheet, and all he hollered at me was, "You're going too slow." Get over in the other lane!" If I hadn't been holding the wheel I probably would have passed out. Seventy was to slow? Oh well, that's California.

In a few weeks I'd be driving just like any other person out there. It was pretty easy. As soon as I learned what exit I needed and where to get on, the in-between I could go like the dickens. That is unless there's all that traffic, and I met that several times.

I also learned what smog was. But going into work was my main thought and I was happy to be back. We had a program rehearsal every Wednesday, Music rehearsal was on Thursday, and then we could go to the dress shop and get whatever we wanted to wear. The show had worked out an arrangement for clothes for us. What we wore was like an advertisement for the clothing companies. We'd have another rehearsal on Friday, then Saturday evening we did the show with an audience. Then we were through until the following Wednesday.

This was very different television than the Jubilee. It was truly a learning experience. Our cast member included Gordon Terry, a great fiddle player and singer; and Freddie Hart, who was just beginning show business. One day, Freddie told me the funniest story about himself. He called himself "Gator Bait." I figured I should ask what it meant. He told me he was born in Louisiana and lived in the swamp. His daddy hunted alligators and when he was little his dad would tie this harness around Freddie and then let Freddie jump off the boat and when the gators came after him, his daddy would pull him in before the gators got him, and then he'd get the gators. I considered this dangerous work, but Freddie just laughed and said, "No danger."

I've seen Freddie in recent years and if I'm with someone who doesn't believe Freddie was "gator bait," I let him tell them. He still always ends the story with "No danger, no danger." Freddie went on to be one of the big superstars in country music, with such hits as "Easy Lovin.'"

As I mentioned, Joe Allison was the MC of "Country America." What a wonderful man he was, then and now. Back then, he was the first radio disc jockey at WSM in Nashville, Tennessee. Before that he toured with Tex Ritter in the 1940s. When Tex quit touring and went back to California, Joe decided to go back into radio in San Antonio, Texas. He met Biff there and helped him to get his start in radio in San Antonio. Later he would come to California to take over Tennessee Ernie Ford's daily radio show and finally he asked to MC the television show "Country America." Still a little later he would be forming a country music department for Liberty Records and I would be one of the first on the label.

I must tell you, under Joe's supervision I did make my best recordings. I talked to Joe a little while back and I asked him about getting the job on "Country America." Why out of all the talent floating around out there was I hired? He told me very simply, number one, he liked my singing; number two, he liked the way I performed and, number three, I was a fine entertainer. What a wonderful compliment. I will never forget it.

[Joe Allison]

We had some more entertainers you would be familiar with, like Jerry Wallace, whose record, "Primrose Lane," was a big hit. A young man named Randy Sparks, who would later form the New Christy Minstrels; Jennie Johnson, a dark-haired beauty; and a cute little girl named Debbie Kaye. Bobbie Bruce was our bandleader and Neal Lavang, who would later join Lawrence Welk, was the lead guitar player. They were all really great musicians and wonderful people to work with. No one on the show seemed to have an inflated ego, so consequently we all got along. With that many personalities together that's really something.

The one thing I loved about the show besides music were all the makeup people. I had my own makeup man and when he got through with my face I felt like I didn't want to take it off. He could make me look great, even on a bad day. When I went anywhere to guest another show I'd always call him and ask what make-up I should use. I was going from no make-up to some make-up and it made me feel good.

One funny thing happened the first time I was on. I always thought my ears were too big, but dad told me that was a sign of generosity. Anyway, by the very first show I hadn't settled on a beauty operator yet, and this operator did my hair in a French twist, so here I am with these big ears sticking out. I asked Orrin, the make-up man, if he could do anything about my problem. He laughed and told me he could tape them back with some spirit gum but he didn't think I needed it done. I convinced him that I did so he taped them back. I believe I did look different.

The girls and I had to stick our heads though a board at the beginning of the show, you know, like a commercial, so we were standing there singing this little jingle and I wasn't bad for the first show. The only thing that worried me was that my ears would come loose and I wouldn't be able to get my head out of the board for my first song. I was singing and thinking about my ears—I know people say you can't do two things at once—and I got tickled. I didn't laugh out loud but I sure did when I got out of that board and Orrin undid my ears. I just decided I'd leave them alone and get another hairstyle.

When I told everyone what I was so tickled about, all of us had a good laugh, the first of many to come. Besides, all that taping back was a little painful. So I let the ears alone.

Unlike the Jubilee, with its rail fences and hay bales, "Country America" had some great sets. You could pick out the song you were going to do at the program meeting, tell a little bit about it, how you'd like to present the song, and if it needed costuming, you could do that too. My favorite song I did in costume was "Oh Lonesome Me." I went into Hollywood to a costume shop and got a skunk outfit, I also got a little civet cat, an unscented real one, from a pet store. The set director and the prop men fixed a woodland scene with tree trunks and all that goes into a forest, and the little skunk and I performed the song. It was a very clever piece of work. I really loved being in costume. There's a side of me that was beginning to emerge in Hollywood that I didn't even know existed. I guess it's called "HAM." Anyhow over the course of "Country America" I began to do several different characters. Joe Allison told me later that he fought the producers of the show to have us really do some good country stuff and get away from the hay bales and rail fences. He felt, as I do, that country people are not hicks and I really believe like he does then and now that we don't need to be talked down to. Just because I'm a yodeler I don't need to sit on a wagon bed to yodel.

Anyhow, country in the mid-fifties was beginning to bloom. We were having good country entertainers like Roger Miller, Ray Stevens and Glen Campbell, who just a little later would be coming on up with good country TV shows. But I had "Country America" and the Little Martin and I was happy just being part of it. And with Biff's help I felt I could become more creative about my TV work.

Biff by this time was still with KLAC radio in Hollywood and on my days off I would get interviews with the stars for his radio show. One interview that he wanted really badly was Groucho Marx, so I just said "I'll get him" and that's what I set out to do. I would just find out who produced his show then I'd call and get an interview with Groucho—so simple, if you've got lots of nerve.

I'll never forget the day I called. It was early for California people but I called and got the producer. We talked and I asked for the interview for Biff, then suddenly the conversation turned around and she, the producer, was interviewing me. I couldn't believe it. She wanted to know who I was, what I did, where I was from, the whole works. Well I'm a talker, as everybody knows. Also, I hardly ever met a stranger, so we chatted on and on. I guess she thought I was

Biff's secretary because I was setting up interviews. I told her that I was his wife and how we came to California and about the "Country America" show and before we hung up she asked me to come to the office and be interviewed for "You Bet Your Life." I was really excited. Being on his show was something I hadn't thought of. I'd seen Groucho in the movies since I was a kid and maybe being on his show, well, WOW!

I couldn't wait for Biff to come home and when he did, he was as excited as I was. Groucho's office wanted me to tell them something about myself that was particularly funny. I thought for a while and the funniest thing I could think of was that I played clarinet in the band in school until they found out that I couldn't read music. What a blast. But it was true. Professor Huckstep didn't know until Lowell Smithson graduated and left the band. I had always copied what Lowell was playing. He was such a super clarinet player.

Let me tell you how I got by without them knowing. I started out at the bottom in the clarinet section and on certain days we had to challenge to move up. I would always challenge someone better, then we'd go in the band room so no one could see and we'd play. I always let the other person go first because they were better and since I had an ear for music I could pick it right up. Then I'd play and the band or Mr. Huckstep would declare a winner. I always moved up. I moved up to the first chair of the clarinets and then my world collapsed. Lowell graduated. I did fine until we had new music. When I couldn't play, Mr. Huckstep asked me what was wrong. I asked to see him in the hall please. When I told him I thought at first he didn't believe me. I had been in the band since grade school and now I was telling him I couldn't read music. I took the easy way out. I decided to leave the band and take another subject. I didn't know that in a couple of months I'd be going to Kansas City to work in radio. Anyway, I exited gracefully.

I'm not saying this is the way things should be done, but for me reading music was a waste of time. Now, I wish I had read. A person needs all the education and learning they can get. Years later when I went to visit Professor Huckstep he told me he still was amazed at my not reading music because I played so well. I told him he was a delightful man and a very good teacher, if you paid attention.

Anyway I decided this was the story I'd tell Groucho's people and I did just that when I went in for my interview. Of course they asked me what I was doing now and I told them I was still playing music, which was funny, only not having to read, and working in television. Needless to say, I was going to be on the show. I was very excited. But this particular event would be maybe two months in my future. So Little Martin and I continued on being creative.

I also began to play the Autoharp and accompany myself on one of my songs, "Oh Yes, Darlin'," which was a pretty good record for me. We used the Autoharp of Mommy Maybelle fame, which gave the song a nice soft sound. Hank Garland played the harp on the record when we went to Nashville to record. Biff would stay up in the control room with Joe Allison and they'd always let me know if things were going all right.

Joe was a wonderful producer. He could make you feel at ease. I'd been trying to figure out lately who was picking my music to record. I'd say probably Joe, because he knew what was making it at the time and how to turn out good records.

I mentioned Hank Garland playing on my records. Hank or Grady Martin were almost always my lead guitar men, with Harold Bradley on rhythm guitar, Jerry Reed on guitar, Bob Moore bass, Buddy Hamm drums and Pig Hargest or Floyd Cramer at the piano. What a lineup! Can you imagine having all these stars of today playing for you? To me they were already stars.

One sad note about Hank Garland. I met Hank when he was working for Eddy Arnold at the Jubilee in Springfield, Missouri. He was such a lovable man. He would sometimes take my girlfriend and me out to dinner if he and Eddy came over early enough before the show. After my recording of "Oh Yes, Darlin'" and "Dime a Dozen" I would never work with Hank again. He had a terrible wreck not far from Nashville and the last time I heard anything about him he was still unable to play ever again. How very sad for such a great guitarist.

To my Friend, Shirley, a wonderful talent and a wonderful lady!! GOD BLESS.... Harold Bradley

[Harold Bradley]

My record of "Dime a Dozen" made me the number three girl singer in country music according to *Billboard* Magazine, one of the "bibles" of country music. This magazine has the charts of where you are according to polls and what your record is doing in the nation. All the entertainers read it. Biff subscribed to all the entertainment magazines. Little Martin and I were really having a good time on "Country America."

As I mentioned, I began to realize that I could do more than just stand up and sing. I could do comedy. I could do skits, too. Maybe I just liked being someone else. I was always getting ideas for songs that required me to go to the costume shop, and that was a lot of fun. I did "Night Train to Memphis" dressed as a hobo. That turned out really well, and I introduced a character named "Quits." This little girl was a younger Minnie Pearl telling "Jimmy Dickens" jokes. I danced and sang **and just** had a great time doing it. They would ask me why my name **was** Quits and I would say, "I came from a big family and when I **was born** Daddy took one look and told Mom let's just call her quits. So Quits was born.

Quits **was** on her own more when I joined "Town Hall Party" after "Country America" ended. I also did "Woodle," which was really me as a little girl. Mom and Grandma Davis sent a clipping out of the paper that they'd kept for years about me. When I was six years old and performed at the Sugar Bowl in Chillicothe, Missouri, I sang "You Must Have Been a Beautiful Baby" and tap danced. We had on the set a piano player for me, and the scene looked like the inside of an ice cream parlor, almost exactly like the Sugar Bowl. I had on a little ruffled dress like I wore and white socks and tap shoes and a great big bow in my Shirley Temple hairdo, and I did my song.

Speaking of Shirley Temple hairdos, that was traumatic for me when I was six years old. My mother and I would always have a time when she combed my hair. It was long and she pulled it like the devil. I would always fidget and fuss so she said, "We'll just have to fix it like Shirley Temple's hair," who was the rage in the movies at that time.

We went uptown in Chillicothe and to the beauty shop for a permanent wave. I can tell you they had a machine in there and when they had rolled up your hair they put these rods down over your hair. It looked like something they would electrocute you with. I was scared silly. Since I can't really describe this machine for you, a friend of mine and a great beauty operator from Mt. Vernon, Illinois, Karen Rowe, has one of these now antique permanent machines and she's promised I can have a picture of it so everyone can see what I went through at such an early age. It's funny now, but it sure wasn't then.

People have asked me where the name "Woodle" came from. There was a cute little girl that my brother used to play with in Chillicothe when we were kids. I don't believe I ever heard any name for her but "Woodle," so that's all we called her. I kind of liked the name "Woodle." I guess I thought it was cute, so my little girl character was named that. Late I would also name a toy poodle "Woodle," as well as a mynah bird that Biff and I would get.

Woodle was a mynah bird that talked. She was really funny. Biff would play taped recordings of us saying "My name is Woodle" and good night and she learned to say hello from us answering the telephone. These birds are so smart. They mimic your voice. It was really something to hear your voice coming from a bird. Several of our entertainer friends came to our house and they thought Woodle was terrific. Even now after all these years they still mention her.

My life with Biff had settled into somewhat of a routine by now. I was working in Hollywood on the television show, doing recordings, trying to keep house and at the same time being supportive of Biff who was still at KLAC. I helped him with his programming and his interviews, as I said, like getting an interview with Groucho Marx.

By now it was just about time for me to meet Groucho Marx. So with my Autoharp under my arm—the producers had decided Groucho and I would sing a duet—Biff and I went to the show. Aunt Mary went along and she and Biff sat in the audience. I didn't know until after the show that Biff had lost his job at KLAC and he was hoping against all hope that I'd win a lot of money. Not that we were poverty-stricken, but every little bit helped.

What I'm going to tell you about the Groucho show may surprise some of you. The directors, producers and the script people had a meeting with all the contestants before the show. At that meeting you met your partner and were allowed to pick out the category you wanted to be questioned about. I really wanted movies, since I was a bit of a movie buff, but someone else had it, so my partner and I, a young man who had been in a motorcycle accident and needed money, and who also was a friend of the producers, picked books.

The script people handed us a script with what we were going to say to Groucho. I read it over and told them I couldn't do that because if Groucho asked me anything I'd just like to tell it like it was. They just told me to do the best I could to follow it because it had quite a few joke lines in it. I had always thought Groucho ad-libbed all the funny lines he said, but unbeknownst to us he was reading from a cue card sheet. Actually it was a cue sheet wall with the whole script printed on it. If you will look at some of the "Best of Groucho" shows now you'll notice that he isn't looking at the contestants, he's reading. So what you see on television is not necessarily what is going on.

I didn't like the idea that we were told to pretend they'd picked us out of the audience and we'd just come on stage, but this was Hollywood and the Groucho Marx Show, so what did I know. I was on the show that millions of people watched and I had a chance to win some money. I had on one of my prettiest dresses, a gray silk of course we didn't have color, with my red hair and by now I'm getting slender, I looked pretty good at least I could hear the audience laughing and applauding. Then it was our turn. Our category was books, which wasn't too bad. Groucho did his introductions to us. He made mention that my last name was "collie like the dog?" I told him yes and then we took off into never never land. I had already said I could not follow a script and at this point Groucho wasn't following anything either. He asked me to tell him a little about myself.

I told him I was a country music singer and a musician. Then I told him my story about being in the school band and not being able to read music. He thought that was very funny. Then he asked me "after you left the school band what did you do?" I said, "I went to work for another band." He really laughed and so did the audience. Then he wanted to know the difference between a country musician and one who read music, I told him that the country musicians could probably read some but not enough to hurt their music. We were off to a flying start. He was saying this to me, asking questions about almost everything, a lot of which had to be edited—remember, this is before tape. Then I said the secret word, which I think, was "house" and that duck or whatever kind of bird it was came down and scared me to pieces. George Fenneman was the announcer and he handed me the fifty-dollar bill, then George tried to turn the show to the question period. Groucho decided to do the same thing. He said a couple of things to my partner about who he was and where he was from, but I simply can't remember his answers. Our first question I will never forget was "The title of the book about a boy and his deer." The answer was "The Yearling." Before I could say anything my partner said "Bambi." I could have choked him. The next question was "the name of the book in which a navy commander is obsessed with strawberries." I didn't consult with anyone. I said "The Caine Mutiny," which was correct. I believe that was the one-hundred-dollar question. The last question was, "What was the name of the captain in Moby Dick." Do you know, I went completely blank? I could not think. I did remember seeing that movie in Harrisburg, Pennsylvania but I could not remember his name was Ahab. So much for the questions. Needless to say we didn't come back for the big money, but later they picked that show to be in the "Best of Groucho" series. Waylon Jennings told me about a year ago that he had just seen it and it was very funny. I thought so too. Biff thought we were funny too but he wished we had made more money. The filming we did that night lasted more than four hours, but believe me the time spent with Groucho was worth it. I really couldn't believe that I was looking at Groucho Marx. The one part I wished they hadn't edited out was when I played my autoharp and Groucho and I sang "Chime Bells" and yodeled with Groucho.

Chime Bells

Out on the mountain so happy and free
There lives a boy and he's wait'n for me
Out on the lake we'll drift with tide
And hear those chime bells ring.
Chime bells a-ring'n
Yodel
Mockingbird sing'n
Yodel
Out on the lake we'll drift with tide
And hear those chime bells ring.

If I could have had a clip of Groucho and me it would have been priceless. I would have treasured it.

After the Groucho show I got a call from the studio casting department to come over. Of course my question was, why me? They needed someone with an accent to be on "Divorce Court," a very popular show during the sixties. Naturally, I went. I found out that I would have to read, which meant they gave you a part of the script and you had to read from it. I was extremely nervous and there were two other women wanting the part, so that meant there was competition but I didn't let all that bother me. If I didn't get the role, everything would still be all right. But this was the first time I had ever read for anyone, so that's why I was nervous.

The role called for the woman to be a western woman, whatever that was. Her daddy owned a riding stable and she had burned the thing down and blamed her husband for it and was trying to divorce him. Not really complicated, was it? Just like the soap operas. Anyhow I just talked the same way I always do and, by golly, I got the part. The casting lady told me I was so sincere about the way I read, and I really read cold, which means I didn't get time to study it. So I had something else to do. In a couple of weeks I'd be on "Divorce Court," which was a very big show in Chillicothe, Missouri.

I think the whole town watched the day I was on just to see how I would do. My husband was played by Joe Allison from "Country America" and we had a real, retired judge, actor lawyers, a real lawyer consultant and a courtroom.

It became very funny when we were doing the show. I was supposed to have been very drunk when I burned the stables down. I was a real bad egg. I was dressed in a cowgirl outfit with boots and a hat, to make me look very "western." At least California western. Every time I looked at Joe I would have to lay my head on the table and cover up my face. I was trying to act ashamed but underneath I was forcing myself not to laugh. We made it through all right and if I remember right the bailiff hauled me off to jail. Good enough for me, right? So much for acting. I decided I would rather sing.

Up to this time I've always mentioned that the Little Martin guitar was always with me and she was—being played by all the wonderful guests we had on our TV show, being carried, I have no idea how many miles. Never forgotten, always remembered. If she could talk, which she can in her own way, she'd tell you of all the good and bad times we've had together. I wrote a song once long ago back in Kansas City about her called "My Guitar" It simply says:

I could never be lonely, I could never be blue.
I'll go through life if only I have a guitar like you.
Why should I worry?
Why should I be sad?
We travel through life in a hurry,
Sharing the good and the bad
Here we go—just you and me,
Oh how happy we will be.
We'll hitch our wagon to a star,
And I'll sing with you,
My old guitar.

Those lines pretty well describe the way I felt about her when she was brand new. When I wrote the song she was sixteen and I loved her even more. I was twenty-six and the year was 1957. Country music was on the horizon everywhere. I was beginning to perform more than just on "Country America." I was doing some personal appearances around California. You know, you could work around that state forever. So, I was doing some more local television shows. Then I get a call to come back to the "Ozark Jubilee" to guest. So being very Californian by then, I loaded up my hairdresser, Joanne, my make-up case, and some beautiful clothes and we boarded the airplane for Kansas City, Missouri.

From there we'd rent a car and drive to the Jubilee. Then we'd go up to Chillicothe to see my folks and then back to Kansas City and home to L. A.

We had some great traveling company on the plane: Dennis " Chester" Weaver, Milburn "Doc" Stone, Amanda "Miss Kitty" Blake, all from "Gunsmoke." Everyone was there but Matt Dillon.

Chester was a riot. He limped up and down the aisle, showing everyone he really walked that way, which he didn't. Miss Kitty and Doc were very subdued and hardly said anything at all. They were going to the Missouri State Fair in Sedalia, so we all had the same plane together.

When we landed in Kansas City, Dad and Mom, Grandma and Mary Lou were there to see us before we went on to Springfield and my dad was more interested in the fact that he'd seen Chester than anyone. Well, not really, but I did tease him some about them. Of course he had an eye for Miss Kitty. Dad always liked pretty ladies. I thought maybe they might go with us to Springfield, but Dad said they needed to get back home because the next day, Saturday, was sale day at the sale barn and he had to work. That meant hauling cattle and hogs that needed to be hauled. Dad had a big business. We were going to see them late Saturday night after the show and so we all said goodbye for a little while. It was really good to see everybody.

[Mary Lou, Me, Dad, Mom]

This time going to the Jubilee was really nice. Sonny James, "The Country Gentleman," was Master of Ceremonies. I'd worked with Sonny before when I was at the Jubilee so it was just like old-home week. The person I really missed seeing was Red Foley, and I really wanted to. He probably would have me sing "Are You Lonesome For Me Annabelle?" I was prepared to sing for him too.

Are You Lonesome For Me Annabelle
Won't you come back to me?
I'm so lonesome you see.
Lonesome for you, Annabelle.
Someone made you feel blue
Said I didn't love you
You know I do Annabelle.

It would be several years before I finally saw Red in Fort Worth, Texas, when I was with Willie.

I was getting to be a pretty good television entertainer and everyone commented on how great I looked. Because to the show in California I had dropped a lot of weight and that meant I would look good on camera.

Actually I was too thin-looking off-camera. I was about 98 pounds. I had weighed probably around 105 when ABC-TV decided I was too heavy. Their reasoning was you photograph on television at least ten pounds heavier than you are. So they sent me to their doctor in Beverly Hills. He prescribed some kind of pills for me to give me energy and made me forget to eat. Sound familiar? I didn't have any idea what I was taking, but the pills really took off the weight. I usually was too busy to eat, anyway. I was only five-feet-two and wore high four-inch-tall heels, called "skyscrapers," so I really looked terribly thin.

I had read an interview someone had done with me and they described me as willowy. I have never thought of a short person as being "willowy." But it sounded wonderful. I did weigh under a hundred pounds so that was skinny for me, or anyone, I guess.

The day after the Jubilee, my folks had a picnic for me and tried to make me and Joanne eat everything in sight. I had a great visit with everybody in Missouri, and then it was time for us to head back to California.

While I was in Missouri, I found out that all the time we were gone it rained out there. Up to this point I hadn't seen any rain or change in seasons in California. Everyone decided that whenever they wanted rain, they'd send me back to Missouri.

When we got back home, Biff had great news. He would be working for KFOX, the country music station in Long Beach. This was a very popular country station out there and one of the best and biggest. His show would come on shortly after noon and run for four hours. That was great for Biff, because he definitely was not a morning person. He liked to start his day around noon. Back when we were on the Phillip Morris Show, he almost missed the bus a couple of times, and that's when he was the manager.

Thinking back on it now, it seems to me the years Biff and I spent together were pretty much like normal folks if you can call two successful careers going at the same time normal. We didn't argue very much—we didn't have time. We were both extremely busy. He was supportive of me and I was the same for him. In fact, on his radio show he was always talking about what "his girl, Shirl" was doing, and I became a personality on his radio program.

Biff was very good about finances, too. All the money I earned on television, plus personal appearances, records or anything I did, was my own. I could put it in the bank and have it for anything I wanted. To me this was great. I'd never in my life been able to do that. I'd always just lived from payday to payday, like any other musician. I was trying to make a living for Grandma and me first, then later just for me, but with Biff I really had someone who supported me.

I really missed Grandma a lot. I had always wanted her to come to California to see us, but she didn't make it. To those in Missouri, California was definitely a faraway place. I'd missed my sister Mary Lou's growing up, and I really didn't know my brother because I hadn't been around him since we were kids. I guess in reality I didn't know my family very well. If you leave home when you're young as I did you miss out on lots of things. Grandma was my cornerstone, as she was when she was with me. Mom would write and tell me the news but we didn't telephone like we do now. So all in my world was

Biff and me and work. His folks came from San Antonio, Texas once or twice and his niece came out to dinner quite a bit. Wonderful places to eat out there, and we visited with Joe and Audrey Allison and always had about four or five New Year's Eve Parties to attend. I remember one New Year's Eve party we went to early in the evening at a beautiful home in Beverly Hills. It belonged to a stunt man Biff had met and when we went into the living room, Guy Madison and his date who looked like Elizabeth Taylor were standing there. I guess I'll never get over being wide-eyed about movie stars. He was so handsome in a green western suit and patent boots. I almost collapsed. I'd seen him in the movies and on television but neither one did him justice. He was such a gentleman too. But then most movie stars I met then were very nice.

I don't really remember any one movie or television star being hateful to me but I'm sure some would rather not be bothered. I remember seeing Kim Novak at the height of her career in the grocery store in Hollywood and she was shopping just like anyone else. Isn't it funny we sometimes have an idea they're not regular people but most of them are or are at least trying to be. As I look back in California into all that has happened so far in the country music business I've seen us go from hillbilly hicks to uptown country.

We went from having very few recordings at all to a pretty big record market. Record companies were beginning to promote country and promote larger departments for us. On my label, Liberty, there was a good country singer, Warren Smith. Joe decided Warren and I should try to do a duet. The night of the recording, which we did in California—you must realize we were recording with live musicians, no tracks—Warren would get so far into the song then look back at me and stop singing. The songs we planned to do were "Why, Baby, Why," an old Webb Pierce, Red Sovine song and "Angel on My Mind." I couldn't for the life of me figure out what was wrong. All of a sudden Warren just walked away from the microphone and into the control room with Joe. Of course everything stopped. In just a little bit Joe came out and told everyone to hold on a few minutes while he talked to me. He took me aside and told me Warren said he couldn't sing with me. I thought things were going good myself so I said, "What's the problem?" Joe told me Warren told him that he thought I was so pretty and such a good singer that every time he looked at me he forgot to sing.

I'd been accused of things before but never for being too pretty. I was flattered. Needless to say Warren did his part, flew home to Texas and in a few days I did mine in California. Some duet. It did well on the market, and got lots of airplay too. If I do say so myself, I thought it was a good record. But after that we didn't record any more. Warren was let off the label, so Joe needed to find me another singing partner. Hopefully one I could look at.

I mentioned live recording a little while back. To me nothing can compare to what we did back then. The musicians sat around, giving their input into the songs. Of course, using tracks was all right. That's where the musicians lay down what they will do on the record that is play their part. Then someone else goes in and plays their part. The producer keeps building until he has exactly what he wants with the music. Then the star goes in whenever it's convenient and sings with the tracks. Most all recording is done that way today. Even to electronic drums. Isn't that something? But I definitely miss everybody standing around laughing and talking and just the fellowship of doing a recording. But you can't stop progress, can you? I heard some drum tracks the other evening and they were fabulous. What will be next, electronic people? That's really funny. Anyway the recording with Warren was over, so back I went to television.

I mentioned Gordon Terry. People who watched "Country America" thought we were brother and sister. He was very good-looking, big and husky and it would have been very nice to have a big brother like him. He was a bit of a lady's man, so I would have to beat the women off so he could sing. But anyway, Gordon had a pet monkey that he carried on his shoulder all the time. I don't remember its name but it was kind of cute if you like monkeys. He had to go to Nashville to record on business or something like that and he decided to take his monkey along. Before he left he gave himself and the monkey a couple of pills to stay awake for the trip. When he got back he was laughing and told us the monkey never closed its eyes one time, he sat there on his shoulder and watched the lights all the way. I guess it didn't hurt the monkey at all he seemed just as happy as he always was. I've been meaning to talk to Gordon and see whatever happened to him and that monkey. I'll bet they had a good time together, because Gordon was really full of fun.

I don't know why this story reminded me of a funny thing that happened to Webb Pierce back at the "Ozark Jubilee" days. He came over from Nashville on Friday evenings and he told me, "The darnedest thing happened." Of course I was always interested about anything and everything so tell me, I said. He told me that the other night there had been a party at someone's house and everybody got pretty drunk. I suppose as the hour got later and later everyone began to pass out except Webb and this fellow who sat across the room from him. This guy was sitting on the floor propped up against a chair with only one eye open. I've seen drunks do that. They close one eye and the other eye stays open. I'm going to have to ask some of my doctor friends why that happens. Anyhow, Webb told me he played the guitar and sang everything he knew and half of everyone else's songs and this guy still just sit there with no emotion.

Finally someone woke up and asked Webb what he was doing. He told them he was trying to sing to this guy across the room and he just wanted to get him to show some emotion. They began to laugh and told him "Webb, you're singing to a glass eye. Webb, that's Radar. He passed out hours ago. Don't you recognize him?" Needless to say, Webb didn't and he ended up staying up all night singing to that glass eye. I told him he'd better check everyone out when he went to a party after that.

Later he thought what he'd done was funny but at the time he told me he didn't act too happy that he'd done something like that. He probably never let Radar go to any more parties where he was. Nashville has always been full of characters, musician entertainers, and the like. Someone always has had a story to tell and over the years you can sure collect a lot of them if you listen. I really don't understand why there were so many there but there just are—about Radar, about Ben Dorsey, who was everyone's busboy and who's with Willie now, trying to be a Willie look-alike.

At this time Jimmy Dean, the sausage king, who, when I reminded him he'd had a television show in New York and played the accordion, told me to shut up and forget it. I also said he had big ears too, like mine, and laughed. He laughed, too. It seemed to me everyone and anyone back then was a character.

As my days in Hollywood lengthened, my days in Nashville did the same and I was meeting more and more people. I flew to Nashville to record and ended up staying with Carl Smith and Goldie at their ranch. I also was a guest on the Grand Ole Opry on Saturday night. It was exciting for me. I'd been to the Opry but never as a guest. I was on Faron Young's segment and I did my yodel song, "He Taught Me to Yodel." The crowd loved it.

The Opry was still at the old Ryman Auditorium and the nostalgia was thick. They had pictures on the wall of all the artists that were members, quite a few of them but not as many as now. There was Roy Acuff, Bashful Brother Oswald, Stringbean, Minnie Pearl, Cowboy Copus, Hawkshaw Hawkins, Ernest Tubb, Little Jimmy Dickens and Grandpa Jones and I'm thinking I get to be on the radio show with them.

What a fantastic event. Ott Devine who was the manager of WSM radio at that time gave me a tape of my part of the show so I could take it home with me. Maybe at one time I thought I'd like to be a member of the Opry, but at that point I didn't pursue it. You must remember that Biff and I were pretty well settled and making good money in California, so I hadn't thought about leaving. I'd appeared with and worked with almost all the people on the Opry over the past few years, so it was like old home week to me. Believe me, the Little Martin sounded like a million dollars and everyone was glad to see both of us.

It's hard to realize that after so many years I still had the same instrument that I had played in Kansas City. She still had the same case and was in mint condition. Up to that point, the Little Martin had been played by so many people and it was hard to keep track of who had played her. I'd never loaned her out—you know, let someone take her for a while to play—but many people had used her on the shows I'd been on. By now she was sixteen years old and I was twenty-six. I always seem to stay ahead of her in age. But that's the way it is.

I remember back at the Ozark Jubilee when a bunch of us had gone to Chicago to appear on Pee Wee King's television show. That group included Chuck Bowers, Jimmy Gately, Harold Morrison, a guitar and banjo duet, Webb Pierce and I and another man named Arlie Duff, who had just written "Y'all Come." Arlie was one of the funniest men you'd ever hope to meet. We stayed at the Planters Hotel not far from Pee Wee's theater. One of Arlie's favorite things was to pick at random from the phone book, someone's name and tell them he had 500 baby chicks to be delivered to them. The person on the other end of the line of course was going crazy, but we all had a good time listening to Arlie convince whoever it was this was for real. Later Gordon Terry would do the same routine with the phone but I think Arlie was the first. Chuck also told us that when Arlie had gas he could play a tune with it. Can you imagine? I never cared to investigate that at all. But as I said everyone was a little crazy in those days.

After my appearance on the Grand Ole Opry, I stayed with Goldie and Carl Smith a few days as I was in the process of looking for some material to record. At this time I met the greatest song-plugger in the world, Hank Cochran. He had just written "I Fall to Pieces" for Patsy Cline, "Little Bitty Tear" for Burl Ives and was a great supporter of a fella I would meet later, Willie Nelson.

Changes on the Way

In about 1961 I decided I had better move into the Andrew Jackson Hotel in Nashville for a day of so, which was more convenient for me since I didn't have a car. Hank phoned and said he'd be over. I'm going to say in my opinion, Hank does not have the greatest voice in the world, but the way he strummed the guitar and presented any song he played made you think it was a hit. I didn't really have the last word on the songs I recorded, but I knew what I could sing. I know I had wondered in the past who picked my material 'cause I know I didn't. By now I have a little input No one bothered to tell me the one bad fault about Hank; he fell in love immediately with the female he was singing to. Maybe that's why he sounded so good. I didn't fall for him, I liked him as a friend, but believe it or not he had a tape of songs I really loved by Willie. I wanted to meet Willie but Hank told me it wasn't possible at that time. Many years later when reading Willie's book I found out that he and Hank had a bet over which one would get around to me first. They had seen a glossy promo picture of me and I guess the both of them were quite taken with it. So maybe this is the reason Hank couldn't find the time to introduce me to Willie. Strange things happen, don't they?

If I had known the bet had happened perhaps things might have been different in my life, but at the time everything was working out according to God's plan. Before I left Nashville I was on Ralph Emery's all-night radio show over at WSM. Their studios at the time were just across the street from the Andrew Jackson Hotel. So I was really a very busy person when I came to town. But within a few hours I'd be on the plane headed back to California and Biff. It was good to be back home to him and Rusty, the peke, and my friends out there. We have a solid life together and we both have successful careers going and it seems nothing at all can bother us.

I found out when I got home that within a few months "Country America" was going to try to go into syndication and leave ABC-TV. So that meant I would need to find something else to do. I was very optimistic about everything and I decided I'd go over and see about joining "Town Hall Party" which was on another great California country show. I had watched the show on television and I knew pretty well what they needed. Me, of course. They had some really great artists on the show: Joe and Rosalee Maphis, Tex Ritter, Merle Travis, Billy Mize, Jeanne Sterling, several comedians and Jay Stewart the announcer. Jay worked at NBC Television and did a lot of very popular shows at the time for Ralph Edwards. Ralph if you recall had such shows as "This is Your Life" and many, many, many game shows. One of the shows that Ralph did was "It could be you" a network television show. Later on I asked him to surprise my grandmother on her birthday. They did and she was tickled. The show even sent her roses too. They would say the person's name and where they lived, so when they said "Mrs. Mata Davis of Chillicothe, Missouri." the whole town was surprised. But anyway, I just take myself over to "Town Hall Party" and get a job. No manager, no agents, no nothing, only myself. They liked my work so the next thing I knew I was back on television.

At the same time I talked with Cal Worthington who had a local show on Sundays and make arrangements to do his show too. Cal's show ran several hours on Sundays, so there really wasn't a problem setting up a time to be on. Cal was one of the largest car dealers in California so his show was extremely popular. At his show one Sunday afternoon, this little lady dressed in western clothes, boots, cowboy hat came up to me and told me how much she liked my yodeling. She hoped I would always continue and never let the way I yodel die. I told her I'd give it my best to do just that. I was totally honored to be talking to none other than Patsy Montana. Patsy's recording of "Cowboys Sweetheart" had sold over a million records in the early 1940s. I had heard her for years but I had never dreamed I'd be meeting her in person. She had made a special trip just to see me. I'd seen her on "Austin City Limits" just a few weeks earlier and she sure was never going to let her part die so neither would I. All of us yodelers have to stick together. We definitely don't want yodeling to become a lost art.

At "Town Hall Party" I was going to give the comedy part of me, "Quits," time to really get out there and do something. I absolutely loved doing comedy and between Minnie Pearl and Little Jimmy Dickens comedy routines I had a world of material. Little Jim came and visited me and Biff and on the way home to San Gabriel he told me "Quits had used all his material" He just laughed and said he'd have to think up some other funny stories. He wasn't mad at all, but he teased me about it. I did some creative bits of my own. Things that I'd done over the years and then the other male comedians and me would get together and put some ideas together, visual things for television.

We were having a ball. Sometimes our comedy routines would go completely through the time we were on the air. So you didn't want to turn off your set if you were watching us. We were really wild and crazy and having lots of fun. When you can enjoy what you're doing it is twice as rewarding.

I believe with all my heart I'd always enjoyed playing music, not only because I made my living that way, but because it's always been a pleasure. One night at "Town Hall Party" I had a call from Charlie Hodge. Charlie at this time was with "Elvis Presley." He was the little guy who always handed Elvis his scarves. But I had known Charlie since the Ozark Jubilee when he was with the Foggy River Boys. He told me "Elvis loves Quits" and he wanted to hear a yodel song. Well, Quits didn't ever yodel. She danced and sang but it was Shirley who yodeled. But if Elvis wanted a yodel, he'd hear one. I was really flattered. So I had to change clothes, Quits was dressed similar to Minnie Pearl, come back on as Shirley Collie and dedicated a yodel song especially for Elvis. Just to know that Elvis was watching delighted me. In fact, Quits was getting better known than Shirley and several times when I was on a personal appearance people would call me Quits. I've talked with several comedians that do an act like this and it sometimes happens when you are playing a role it takes over.

So I'm going to have to think more Shirley than Quits. Kind of confusing isn't it?

Life was proceeding along at a fast pace. Biff was exceptionally busy and becoming well known in the radio business and I might add very influential and as you already know I'm working as hard as I can on records, television and personal appearances. I believe that in my life I've just about met everyone, in fact some of my friends always laugh when I see someone, I almost always say, "I know you, don't I?" I guess it is funny. At this point in my life, my health wasn't as good as it should be. I seemed to run down quite a bit, from exhaustion mostly. But who wouldn't be. I would have to go in the hospital for three or four days to get my energy back. Biff usually brought something for me to autograph for the disc jockeys all over the country. Pictures or post cards or something like that. I say he did that until the doctors made him stop. When the doctors said rest, that's what he meant.

California doctors were really a different breed to me. They seem always to be looking for something wrong. The last doctor I had out there was determined that my hospitalization was more than just exhaustion that he began making blood tests after blood test while I was in there. I wanted Biff to tell me what in the world was going on. He finally told me the doctor thought I had Lupus and I immediately knew there was no cure for that. Talk about going downhill. I felt my world had fallen apart. Here I am with a successful career, a great husband and all of a sudden the doctors tell you, you have Lupus. This meant the doctors had no idea how much longer I'd live or if I would live. I showed all the dreadful signs and everything pointed that way. Needless to say, I just lay down. Everything I was doing went on hold. I really can't begin to tell anyone how I did feel. Awful isn't really descriptive enough. If you've ever been faced at all with anything like this then you can sympathize with me. I just couldn't get it through my head I might not be living much longer. Biff did everything he could do to make me feel better and keep my spirits up, but until I would come to grips with this I wasn't going to be any good.

At this time we went to Nashville for the disc jockey convention and the CMA Awards and also the BMI dinner. I wasn't going to go but then I decided I couldn't feel any worse there than in California. The only thing that bothered me was Biff would end up telling all our friends about me and that would matter. But then I suppose everyone was wondering why I wasn't my old full of pep Shirley. We did have a good time anyway. Biff was very busy getting his interviews with all the entertainers. The stars would all gather in the Andrew Jackson Hotel in the afternoon and you could always see and talk to just about anyone you wanted. If you'd never been to the disc jockey convention of a few years back, you've never lived. All the rooms in the hotel would be filled by the record companies as hospitality rooms so you could go by have something to drink, eat and visit for a while. The rooms that weren't taken by the record companies were filled by entertainers or someone who had the good fortune, or maybe a better word would be foresight to reserve themselves a room the year before.

Anyway, during this time about everyone was in town for the convention. As I said it concluded with the Country Music Awards or BMI show, the show where all the songwriters were presented with awards for their fine songs being written. After meeting Hank and listening to many other songwriters I suddenly after all these years began to understand the lyrics to the song. For me this is one of the greatest things that ever happened. I'd heard lines in songs that would just knock me out, Marty Robbins sang terrific songs, just to name one, but now I'm really beginning to listen to the words. I'm going to find out a few years later from Biff that he didn't listen to the words either. But I believe the years of the country songwriter are coming around due to Hank Cochran, Willie Nelson, Roger Miller, Harland Howard, just to name a few. I read a couple of days ago in a magazine that after 1941 when Ernest Tubb began using an electric guitar on his record "Walking the Floor over you" that country music made a drastic change. Up to this time, we hadn't used electric instruments, only acoustic. The blue grass groups, like Bill Monroe, will never change. I guess Ernest Tubb led the way to the future. So even way back then just as the war started things were changing. I had occasion to tell Ernest that I remembered him from the movies. He was such a nice man onstage and off. The movie had Ernest and his band, The Troubadours, going all over the country in a big white touring car, no top on it just wide open. They'd stop and sing and play, then move on. He told me he didn't think anyone would remember that, but I did. The people in Hollywood did quite a few movies on Ernest Tubb, Roy Acuff, Judy Canova and country folks. Though probably if I'd see them now they'd look like hillbillies. But when I was back in the Grand Theater in Chillicothe, they sure seemed like everyday folks to me. I loved Lulu Belle and Scotty. They sang and played the banjo and guitar. I sure had hoped then that someday I'd be up there on the screen with them. But back then I was always dreaming. As far as my dream had taken me was to the road, radio and television. If you look at those accomplishments, that's a pretty good dream. At this minute I'm in Nashville and I'm hoping this Lupus thing is just a bad dream. I'll wake up and it will not be true. You hear more about Lupus this day but then I'd never heard anything about it. I'd find out that it's a blood problem and there is no cure just a gradual worsening in strength, so I really had a lot on my mind.

After seeing everybody we hadn't seen since moving to California, we spent an extra day with Carl Smith and Goldie Hill, from the Phillip Morris Show, at their ranch. We figured we'd better get on home and take care of business. Get back to our careers. Even though I was going through quite a bit of stress at this time I found it better to try and stay as busy as I could. Once in a while my energy would completely give up on me and I'd be in bed a couple of days. Other than these problems I still kept on with the Town Hall Party shows and Cal Worthington's show on Sundays. I had made up my mind I was too much of a survivor to just lay down. I kept going to my doctor and he started B12 shots and other medications to help build me up. I believe in the back, top or front of my head there is something that always keeps me going, no matter what. I do believe it is God and He's never gonna let me give up on me. I'll fight everything and anything with God's help. I've talked to other entertainers about health problems, which we all have, and they believe the same as I do. We're tough folks. If you can imagine being on the road and in cars with five other people, and no regular sleep time, and whatever food you can get, we're all lucky to be alive. When someone passes me in a big silver eagle bus like Willie's with all kinds of food, television, bathroom, dressing space and a bed to sleep in, I believe it's got to be truly heaven. If we had been asked in the late forties if we thought this would happen, naturally we would have said you were crazy. No one at that time envisioned country music going as far as it has. But no one ever thought country artists would be making as much money as they do now either.

When I got to thinking a while ago about dressing space, back in the old days, I've dressed in some pretty weird places. Under a stage, with a blanket held around me, in rest rooms, in rooms so small you could hardly turn around. And at this time I'm wearing about three or four stiff petticoats under my skirts. In rooms with no mirrors, in a car, now that's really a deal because you have to put something over the windows, maybe someday I'll get a medal for dressing in weird places, but today it's definitely not the way. They usually have all these beautiful mirrors and great rooms to rest in before your show. How sweet it is. But since I didn't know any different in the old radio and Phillip Morris days everything was just fine. I was working and that was all that mattered.

After "Country America" had closed, someone over at another television station in Los Angeles asked Biff to be Master of Ceremonies for this show and of course I was on it as one of the girl singers. We did all of our own make-up and used our own clothes. It wasn't programmed as well as Country America. It did all right for a while. We had people like Roger Miller and Billy Strange, a wonderful guitar player and singer. He did the famous record for Nancy Sinatra "These Boots Are Made For Walking" and he and I did several radio jingles together.

As I said earlier, Hollywood was about to become a haven for Nashville writers for a while. One of those was Hank Cochran. He had invited me to lunch with him in Hollywood, so I drove in from

San Gabriel and met him at his motel. A couple of guys were playing cards on one of the beds, I knew Roger Miller, we had met before, but the other fella I didn't know. I did notice he had a nice smile and pretty auburn hair and a very quiet manner. Hank introduced me briefly to Willie Nelson. I do mean briefly. The next minute after hello, we were out the door.

Hank said we needed to stop by a recording studio that was close. Joe Allison was recording some of the new country people for Liberty and we needed to drop off some songs. By the time we got there it was really busy in the studio, musicians tuning up and getting ready to do their best with the songs. Hank pretty well kept me isolated from whatever was happening until my curiosity got the better of me. There perched on a stool was this good looking guy Willie Nelson. He started to sing and I started to listen. I'll never forget the first song I heard him singing "Mr. Record Man." I asked Hank if we could stay around for a while and he told me this session didn't mean anything. He was just in a hurry to put some distance between Willie and me. Willie was cutting his first album for Liberty, "And Then I Wrote," and he surely had written a bunch of great songs. Anyway, Hank and I went on to a nice quiet lunch and he presented some new material to me for my next session in Nashville. At the time I didn't know they had a bet about which one would get me first. And I do mean get me. But I belonged to Biff Collie and there wasn't anyone ever going to change that situation, I thought.

Hank went back to Nashville, Willie went on back to work for Ray Price and the Cherokee Cowboys and I went back to Town Hall Party and the Cal Worthington and the straight and narrow life Biff and I were building for ourselves in California. I did go ahead in my mind and deal with the issue of Lupus. I was going to live each day to the fullest and be the best I could be in everything I did.

Fate Steps In

There were definitely many changes about to happen in my life. One of the biggest and most dramatic changes was going to happen to Biff and me. His name was Willie Nelson and he fronted the band of the Cherokee Cowboys for Ray Price.

But let us go back to October 1959 and to the Riverside Ballroom on a Saturday night. As I said before, Biff liked to work on Saturday night, and on this particular night I wasn't going to go with him; but he finally persuaded me to go. For some reason, I had the night off from the Town Hall Party and I was just going to sit around, eat junk food, and watch old movies. But Ray Price and the Cherokee Cowboys were appearing and I liked Ray. So, at last, I got all dressed up.

I remember exactly what I wore, a brown knit dress with a matching long knit jacket of shades of brown and orange. With my auburn hair, those colors went very well. I wore my high, high skyscraper heels, which made me look taller than I really was. I was still extremely thin and thought I looked pretty good. So, on I went to Long Beach and Riverside.

Of course, the place was completely full of people and there was quite a few people back stage just visiting. The Cherokee Cowboys were already on when we arrived. Biff went over to talk to someone about introducing Ray, and I wondered over to the stage curtain and just sort of peeked out. When I did, this redheaded guy playing the electric bass, who was dressed in a pale green cowboy suit, peeked back at me and smiled. He smiled and I smiled back. Then I continued to stand there for a minute or two. I am a very friendly person, especially with my buddies the musicians. I guess I was trying to figure out how I knew him, or if I knew him.

I walked over to Biff and asked him if he knew who the boss-man was. He checked it out and told me, "That's Willie Nelson and he's just about the greatest song writer around today. One of these days, you're going to be able to hear his music everywhere." Biff also told me he was going to ask to interview him for his radio show. I again went back to the curtain and stood there while Willie did a jazz version of "San Antonio Rose." Talk about far out! I had never heard anything like it before. I thought he was absolutely terrific, and could he, Willie, ever play that bass. I noticed he played with a pick. I'd always just played with my thumb, but his sounded great.

In fact, all of the Cherokee Cowboys sounded great! Jimmy Day was playing the steel guitar; Pete Wade was on the electric guitar; Willie was on the bass; and the rest of the guys were really making music. Ray Price had always been known to have a terrific bunch of guys, but these musicians were just super. I was really glad Biff had persuaded me to come along. When they took their break, before Ray came on, they were all backstage. Willie walked directly to me with that same smile, and when he looked at me with those piercing brown eyes he has and took hold of my hand, he said, "Hi, I'm Willie Nelson. You should record some of my songs."

I had a feeling like I'd never had before in my life. I know that I said something back to Willie, but it probably didn't make any sense. He was looking at me and I was looking at him and never thought there were other people around. It was like we were all alone. I will never forget that moment till the day I die! It was like a big light bulb came on over my head and, as I would later tell Willie, "I loved you then and he said he knew, he felt the same way about me."

If you've never experienced anything like that in your life, I hope that someday it will happen for everyone. Such a feeling is so hard to describe. True love? Standing in front of me in a pale green cowboy suit was the man I knew I loved. But the man I was married to and loved was getting ready to go on stage to introduce Ray Price. I was extremely upset. Where was my mind anyway? This just couldn't be happening to me. I came back to my senses, back to where and who I was.

Willie told me he'd see me later and went back out to play for Ray. I walked again to the curtain and stood like I was in a trance. I tried to shake off the feeling that I had, but it seemed that nothing I could do would make it go away. At this time in my life, I had my feet planted on solid ground. I was Mrs. Biff Collie, whose morals could not be questioned. I was Shirley Collie, a successful country music singer who had followed the straight path for more than a number of years. So all of these strange feelings just had to be silly. Maybe I was sick! But whatever it was, I'd be able to figure it out later. I did figure out that I'd seen Willie before, but just in passing, when Hank Cochran invited me to lunch in Hollywood. There, I realized Willie was recording for Liberty just like I was. I'd seen him in the studio, too, but he sure didn't have the effect on me that he'd had just a while ago.

Well, needless to say, I was ready to go home to the safety of San Gabriel. Words just cannot express the way I felt. I watched Biff perform and, when he was through, I asked him if we could go home. He told me we had to wait until the show was over. The reason was that he had invited Willie to go home with us and spend Sunday at our house. Ray wasn't working and Biff would interview Willie and I could cook dinner, and we'd all just relax. Then on Monday morning, after he'd gone to work, I could take Willie back to his motel because Ray was playing the Palomino Club Monday night. I tried to be very composed about the whole idea. I'm not sure exactly how I looked, but I knew one thing—I was going to try and discourage the feelings I'd had whirling around in me.

The club closed about 1:30 or 2:00 A.M. and Biff, Willie, and I climbed in our little Renault and took off for home. I made Willie a bed on the divan and he and Biff talked for a while. I went on to bed. I'd left a pan of beans to soak all night. Biff liked beans and corn bread so much and he liked not to have to hurry when he ate, so sometimes we had them on Sunday. That would be the menu for tomorrow or today, whichever it was right then. All I wanted to do was to fall asleep and wake up being myself again, not like I was at the Riverside Ballroom.

Morning had already come, and since I'm an early riser, I was up and around before either Biff or Willie woke up. Biff was a late riser on his day off anyway, so it would be late afternoon before either of them got up. I puttered around in the kitchen and made some kind of dessert, peeled the potatoes, for fried potatoes, of course, and after I had everything ready, Rusty, my peke, and I went outside. Aunt Mary's yard was beautiful. She had all kinds of flowers and plants, and, as I remember, it was a beautiful day. From our house you could see the mountains and I really liked that. Maybe I was trying everything I knew to stay out of Willie's way. I suspect that's very true.

But it was a small house and sooner or later the three of us would finally be together. By this time, Biff and Willie were awake and wanted something to eat. We bypassed breakfast and went right into the beans and corn bread after they had been up a while. Willie and Biff did the interview. Willie and I exchanged small talk but not about anything really important. He told me he'd been a fan of mine since the Ozark Jubilee and he loved my first record, "Where Did the Sunshine Go?" for ABC Paramount.

I was impressed that such a fine writer would be impressed by me. Biff went on and on to Willie about how great he'd be someday and the day progressed into the evening and Biff asked Willie to stay over again and we'd go bowling later that evening. Willie said that he didn't have anything to do but sit around the motel, so he'd like that. The next day I would take Willie to his motel like they had planned. It seems to me that a lot of plans were being made and nobody was asking me what I thought. But that's pretty normal when you're a wife. Besides, I liked having company. I just wasn't sure if this was the kind of company I should be having. I will have to tell you I was so attracted to Willie, as most people are when they see or meet him, but believe it or not, I was really trying to turn things around. Somewhere along the line, Biff and Willie decided when we came to Nashville for the Disc Jockey Convention, that Willie and his wife Martha would escort us around. Willie was going to get a BMI award for "Hello Walls" and we'd all be together there.

I learned that Willie was married and had three small children living in Nashville. Martha was a good-looking Cherokee Indian and Willie made a joke and said, "Every night with her was Custer's last stand." Neither Biff nor I pursued that remark. You could tell from just listening to Willie talk that he wasn't very happy.

Anyway, the three of us went bowling. Biff was a great bowler. He bowled on a league once a week and he'd gotten me started. I made some impossible shots, no style just luck, and everyone laughed. Willie had a couple of beers and, by this time, it was time to adjourn for the night. I must say again that I was still fascinated by Willie. But the comparison between Willie and Biff was like day and night. Willie had auburn hair and was rather small; Biff had black hair and was just a little bit stocky—not fat, just built well. As I write this, it seems to me I was doing a lot more comparing than I ever thought I had done.

When we got back to the house, Willie played the little 00018 Martin and went on and on about what a wonderful guitar it was. I told him that Merle Travis had named her "Lady" guitar, but Willie said she felt more like a "Baby." In just a few months, that would be the name that would stay with her forever. But for the moment, she was still "Lady."

[Willie's note about the Martin]

Willie played some of his new songs that knocked both Biff and me out. He promised that next time I recorded he'd have something for me. I told him to just give it to Joe Allison since he was producing both of us. I was trying to get away from Willie. Again, I went on to bed while Biff and Willie sat up a while in Biff's studio talking. If there was one thing Biff liked to do, it was talk. This had really been some weekend for me and I knew that after Biff left for work I'd be taking Willie over across town to the Palomino Club and that would be the end of that. Whatever it was, we'd be meeting Willie and Martha in Nashville later. But at the time, it didn't seem like a problem to me.

The next morning I was up early and in the kitchen drinking coffee listening to the radio just like I always did. Biff would be getting ready to leave shortly, then Willie and I would be leaving. We all did have coffee together. As I recall, Willie didn't care for coffee, but he had some anyway. He was telling Biff what a great time he had and how nice it was to be invited to someone's home when you're on the road. Biff and I said goodbye and that we'd see each other after work, and he left for Long Beach. Then Willie said "Why don't you have another cup of coffee, then we'll leave." The radio was playing some slow song and Willie took hold of me and laughed and said, "Let's dance." We both laughed and I said "I think we'd better get on our way, don't you."

When we got on the freeway, we both were pretty quiet. I felt like I wanted to take hold of him, but I knew I shouldn't. So, we did some small talk and I told him what a responsible person I was. I had a good job, TV shows, a wonderful husband, security, and that Biff and I had been together since the Philip Morris show and we were doing well. He really didn't say very much at all for a long time, and then he said, "It sure is strange how things happen. You can be so attracted to someone and love them and not know them at all. Isn't it?" I knew exactly what he was talking about, our meeting back stage at Riverside. I didn't let him see my face too much, but I did say, "Things sometimes happen that people have no control over." He told me that he and Martha didn't get along and he was going to get a divorce.

When we got to his motel, he asked me to come in and I told him I couldn't stay but for just a few minutes. I didn't want to get caught in traffic going back home. But I did go in. He had some phone calls waiting for him. I found out later that he was talking with Martha. She wanted to buy a new car and a diamond ring, and he told her to get them both. That's Willie for you. I knew he was going to have royalties from his songs coming in because he and Biff had talked about it, and I just thought that this was one generous guy. I told him I had to get going and he took hold of me and gave me a really tender kiss on the lips. He said, "I've been wanting to do that ever since I saw you." I didn't say anything, but I felt that kiss all the way home. I did tell him that Biff would call when we got into Nashville and I gave him our phone number at home. He said he had asked Biff for it, but that he had forgotten to give it to him. I left but I didn't really want to. I believe I was just a little bit miserable too. I was afraid of what I shouldn't do and what I might do. The one the one thing I knew was that I wouldn't hurt Biff under any condition. But I figured I'd get over all of this. Wrong! This was just another beginning!

I listened to Biff on the radio going home and he was talking about Willie Nelson and "his girl, Shirl," and what a good time all of us had ever the weekend. All I wanted to do was get home and stop thinking about Willie Nelson. San Gabriel was getting closer, but my mind was at the Palomino Club with the redheaded bass player. I knew Ray Price was going to be in the California area for the next week or so, and he was scheduled for the Cal Worthington TV Show before they went back to Nashville. But I didn't really believe I'd hear from Willie again. Wrong again!

One week later, on a Saturday night, Biff had gone to work again and I was watching old movies on TV when the phone rang. I heard some money drop, lots of background noise, and then this voice saying to me, "Shirley, I love you" and I was saying the same thing back, "I love you too." It was Willie screaming at the top of his lungs. I guess he figured I couldn't hear him, but I could. Then he said, "I don't know what's going to happen, but we'll just work things out some way. I'll see you next Sunday at the TV show." We said, "I love you" to each other again and then hung up.

At intermission he had gone to the phone and called me from somewhere in California where they were playing. I lay back down on the divan and just lay there like I was in shock. Willie Nelson had just said he loved me and I said I loved him too.

The bad part about this was that I did love him. I didn't even think about the "we'll work it out" part. I'm sure people are wondering how in the world I can remember what everyone said back then, but when something happens to you like this you'll never forget one word no matter how long it's been. It seems just like everything happened yesterday. I tried to get myself together. Those last words, "I'll see you Sunday," were ringing in my ear over and over. He meant the Cal Worthington Show. I had no special time I went on to sing, I just went over and appeared once early in the day and then later in the afternoon. But in my head, I wasn't thinking at all about being on television. I was thinking about seeing Willie.

I believe though, when all the things happened to Willie and me, that he was completely in love with me then and sincere about his feelings. The bet he and Hank were supposed to have is still difficult for me to understand and when I am finished telling you everything we went through to be together, it's really hard to believe. To just go to bed with someone shouldn't have caused all the trouble we had.

Waiting a week to see the man you've fallen in love with and trying not to show your feelings, as I am prone to do, to the man you're married to, was one of the most difficult times of my life. I just tried to be calm and cool and go about my life as I'd been doing. I've often wondered if I'd had someone to confide in, a close friend, family or just anyone I'd trusted, if I'd still have been in love with Willie. The answer I keep getting is "yes." I suppose I'm just wasting time thinking about it. Anyway, at that time, I wasn't confiding in anyone.

When I got to the television show, Ray's bus was just pulling out. They'd been on really early and my heart sank to the ground. Then all of a sudden, this red head poked out a window on the side of the bus, and it was Willie. He said, "I really mean what I said on the phone, I love you, and I'll see you when you come to Nashville. Don't ever forget that I love you!"

He was still hanging out the window as the bus pulled away. I yelled back, "I love you, too!" Some of the crew from the television station was standing there looking at me like I'd slipped a cog— Shirley Collie yelling after a bus, I love you! But I didn't care. California people do crazy things.

In a little over a week Biff and I would be going to Nashville and I'd finally get to talk to Willie. How? I didn't know for sure, but if love prevailed, we'd figure it out. When a person wants time to fly by, it doesn't. The week went so slowly. I wonder now if Biff ever noticed any difference in me. I tried not to talk about Willie. Biff did. He asked me what I thought of him and I really don't know what I said. I probably didn't say much of anything, just that he seemed nice and he was a great songwriter. Biff told me he thought he was having lots of trouble at home and some financial problems too, but that with his royalties coming in, he had to be able to straighten things out.

Willie did tell me he had three little children, two girls and a boy. You know, I really wanted to meet them. Later I'd be accused by some people of breaking up his family, but I didn't. It was already beyond repair before I came along. I told Biff that I was looking forward to going to Nashville. Biff always did a great many interviews with the country stars at that time and I would be seeing many old friends. Biff told me that Martha and Willie would be taking us around to the BMI dinner and to the award show, and he was to call them just as soon as we got there. Willie had given him his number at home and he and Martha would be waiting for us. Can you even imagine how I felt? Confused, mainly! This trip could have turned out to be my biggest nightmare.

When we got to Nashville on Sunday evening, we began to relax and have a good time like we usually did. Biff did call Martha and made arrangements with her about picking us up for the BMI dinner on Wednesday night. I guess I should explain that BMI stands for Broadcast Music International. They tell the writer how many times their song has been broadcast and collect a royalty. Every year the writers whose songs have been played the most that year receive recognition awards. Sometimes one writer may get two, three, four or more awards. It's a black tie event. There is a cocktail party before, then dinner and the awards.

Frances Preston, a very lovely lady, was the president of BMI. I had a couple of days to wait until I could see Willie, and I knew when I did see him that we wouldn't be able to talk about what we needed to talk about; namely US! But Wednesday evening came and Biff and I waited in front of the hotel. This big black Cadillac pulled up and Willie got out and started shaking hands with Biff. He opened the car door for me and introduced me to Martha. She was a very beautiful black-haired woman dressed in a pale blue strapless evening dress. She had draped a mink stole around her neck and on her hand was the diamond ring Willie had told her on the phone to go ahead and buy. I wore a simple black velvet sheath with a matching velvet coat and no other piece of jewelry except my silver wedding ring. I was never really big on jewelry anyway, so someone else wearing diamonds didn't bother me at all. At the time, I didn't even wear earrings, just plain old me!

I noticed that Martha gave me some funny looks once in a while during the evening. Not funny, ha ha, but "this is my man, so leave him alone" type of funny. She wasn't telling just me, she was telling everyone. At the cocktail party, everyone was milling around like they usually do. I just sat in one spot and let people come by me; it's easier that way.

Biff was milling around, as usual, talking and seeing all of his friends. Every once in a while, he'd come back to me and we'd talk a little, but I didn't expect him to do that. He knew he didn't have to. Then Willie walked up. He stood in front of me for a moment, then moved to the side and, in a very low voice, told me I looked beautiful. He also said that he knew I was going to have to stay over after the convention and record. That was something I didn't expect. Joe Allison hadn't told me, but I really wasn't surprised since I did record in Nashville, which wasn't out of line. Anyway, he said that he'd see me after Biff went back to California.

We all sat at the same table for dinner and honestly, Martha was a very beautiful woman. You could certainly tell she was Indian, Cherokee, in fact. The only thing I noticed about her was that she drank a little too much, and Willie mentioned that to her a couple of times. But as far as getting along together, they seemed to be doing all right. After the awards, we all stopped by the Andrew Jackson Hotel where almost everyone stayed. It was a little too noisy, so Biff told Willie we'd just walk back to our hotel up on the corner. They left us and later I found out that Willie got really drunk and sent Martha home while he stayed in town. They probably had a fight about that, I'm sure.

Anyway, Biff and I walked back to the hotel and, on the way, he told me I was going to have to stay in Nashville to record and he'd be going on back to California on Sunday afternoon. The rest of the convention went very well and Biff flew back to California with lots of interviews for his radio show. We figured I'd be coming home in just a few days, so everything was going, as it should; except for the fact that I hadn't seen Willie.

I had talked to Joe and he said he'd get back to me sometime Monday afternoon and let me know what time we recorded. When Joe called me later, he asked me to come by his hotel and we'd go over a few songs. When I did go by, he had a visitor, in fact, a couple of visitors—Hank Cochran and Willie. My heart was in my mouth when I saw him. He was still having the same effect on me that he had in California. We managed to pick out some songs for the session and then I said I'd better get on back to my room. Willie said he'd walk with me, as he had to get on home. I doubted that, but it was a good excuse. Then we left. We made our walk a very slow one and several times we stopped to talk. It really wasn't all that far, but I remember everything he said to me. He told me that in a week or so, Ray Price was going to be playing Atlanta and he wanted me to be there. He'd have three days off after they played, then they'd be going out on some more jobs. How in the world was I going to arrange to be in Atlanta, Georgia?

This was what he planned. He would book me on the show as the girl singer and pay me one thousand dollars. Well, he didn't have a thousand dollars at that time. I knew that, but he'd give me a check and I'd take it back to California with me. What did I think of that idea? After he kissed me on the way back to the hotel, what do you think I thought? I wanted to be with him more than anything in the world. Any time or any place, it just didn't matter.

He came on up to my hotel room and stayed a while. We held each other and talked about being together and not really understanding what had happened to us. I've got to believe he meant it because I know I did. I knew people were going to get hurt over our being in love, and some people certainly were not going to understand. But at the moment, the only person I had to answer to was me.

I read somewhere that Martha said he stayed with me all night at my hotel, but he didn't. He probably went on down to Tootsie's or found Hank and they went somewhere. But he didn't stay with me and we didn't make love. Not that we didn't want to, but we didn't.

The next day I recorded. The day after, I flew back to California with a plan. After I got settled in back home and Biff had come home from work, I told him Willie had called. That wasn't a lie; he had called to see if I was all right and if we were still going through with our plan. I told Biff that Willie had convinced Ray to book a girl singer with them in Atlanta for three days and they had decided on me. This wasn't anything out of the ordinary. I'd done lots of personal appearances my entire life. The only thing wrong was that it wasn't true. The three days would be spent with Willie.

Anyway, Biff asked what kind of money they were paying, whether or not I wanted to go, and all the other questions that come up when someone is booking you. I told him and he said he thought the money was fine. One thousand dollars for three days seemed fair and if I wanted it, he said I should take it. He said that he would check the airline for me and see what kind of flight I could get. We had a travel agency that got all our airline tickets for us so that really wasn't a problem. I told him to let me think about it for a while. I hadn't been to Atlanta since the Philip Morris Show and I knew it would be beautiful in the fall. It would especially be beautiful because Willie was going to be there. This would be the first time since I married Biff that I would lie to him. But later on, I found out that it wouldn't be the last.

I made my hotel reservations in Atlanta and packed my suitcase. Of course, "Lady Guitar" had to go along, too. I probably could have gotten by without taking her, but then nothing could look out of the ordinary. I remember that Biff took me to the airport and waited until the plane left. I had forgotten that there was a several-hour time difference between California and Georgia. By the time I got there,

Willie would already be performing. I got my car and I knew when Ray was supposed to be playing and so I just drove right to the auditorium.

Needless to say, I was totally excited. I had been so excited on the flight and I wanted the plane to go faster. Biff had asked me to please call when I got there, so there were several things that I had to do. I thought I'd tell Biff I had forgotten about the difference in the time and had gone directly to the show so I wouldn't miss Ray and I needed to get all that done before I called home. Well, part of that was correct. I really wasn't all that interested in seeing Ray.

When I got to the auditorium they hadn't gone on yet and Willie was in the dressing room. I asked someone if they'd go get him for me and he came running out and just nearly hugged the breath out of me. He said, "You did it, didn't you?" I couldn't answer because I was so happy to see his face. By this time the band had come around. Everyone was saying hello to me. Then Ray walked up and said, "I'll be darned Shirley, what are you doing in Atlanta?" I told him I had some business in town and I had heard that he was there and come to see him. I wasn't sure if he knew that I'd come to see Willie or not. But later on, Ray would become an ally of mine; not that he really took any side. Maybe I should say that he just understood when someone was in love. Anyway, Ray Price was very good to me and Willie!

As soon as the show was over, Willie told everyone he was staying in Atlanta and he'd see them all at the next job. No one said anything then, but I always wondered if anyone said anything on the bus. I guessed probably not. Willie and I loaded his things in the car and headed for the motel. We didn't stay where I had reservations. It really wasn't much of a place like it was supposed to be. Instead, we went to the Downtowner Motel Hotel in Atlanta and I got a small suite and Willie got a room next to mine. So if anyone did enquire, I was staying alone. Biff had some friends at the radio station there and I told him I'd contact them for him. So there were things I had to do. We did stay together that night. It was almost two or three o'clock in the morning by the time we got checked in and by the time we got to bed we were exhausted.

The trip to Atlanta from California hadn't been any small thing, and Willie was very tired from being on the road. So we just lay in each other's arms and talked and kissed, then we both got very quiet. It was almost daylight before we fell asleep. It seemed as if Willie and I had always been together. I remember that one time he did tell me that he thought we were soul mates. We'd been searching for years and finally found one another, even if it was only for three days. But those three days were heaven for me. We talked and talked, we went riding in the car to see the beautiful fall colors in Atlanta; we ate until we were nearly sick, we laughed, and we ran around town after the stores had closed and looked in the windows. We were just like two kids in love.

I had never done anything like that before and Willie said that he hadn't either. Then we began to get serious and started talking about what was going to happen to us because, whether we liked to believe it or not, in a short time this would be ending. We discovered that this wasn't just some crazy fling, but that we really wanted to be together always. How were we going to work things out? That was the problem. My idea was to just tell Biff the way it was. Just tell the truth and everything would be all right. But that may sound good, but it isn't what a person should do. I'll explain that part a little later.

Willie had told me he was going to get a divorce. He'd had lots of trouble for a long time and he felt it was time for some happiness. He told me about his children Lana, Susie, and Billy. The fighting between him and Martha was really getting to the kids, even though they were still small. In Willie's first book that he wrote years and years later, Lana said, "even as a small child, she had wished Daddy and Mommy had divorced so they could be happy." Out of the mouths of babes!

[First bus: Billy, Lana, Willie, and Susie]

Lana was always so grown up to be so little. But she had been through quite a bit at such an early age. I felt I should be completely honest with Willie, and I told him the doctors in California had said I had lupus and I told him a little bit about it; at least as much as I knew. I also told him the way I'd set my head about it and I wasn't going to ever give up, to just lay down and die. I believe that he thought all the love we had, even at that time, could cure anything.

He told me his mother, Mother Harvey he called her, and stepfather Ken, lived in Eugene, Oregon. His dad, Ira, and stepmother, Lorraine, lived in Fort Worth. But he really wasn't all that close to either of his parents. His sister, Bobbie and her husband Paul, and Momma Nelson, also lived in Fort Worth with Bobbie's boys Randy, Mike, and Freddie. Willie was close to Bobbie because they'd been through a lot together. He also said that he hoped someday I'd meet her, and I hoped so too. Then I told him all about

Chillicothe and my folks, especially Grandma Davis. He said that Grandma Davis reminded him a great deal of Mamma Nelson.

Momma Nelson was his grandmother. She and his grandfather had cared for him and Bobbie when his dad and mom divorced. In fact, they had taught him to read music and be interested in music even when he was so small. Later I would learn the song "Family Bible" was a direct result of his upbringing by them. What a wonderful song!

Our three days were over much too soon for the both of us. My plane would be leaving for California before his, so I knew when it came to saying goodbye; it was going to be hard to do. We decided that he would call and let me know where he would be when Ray came back out on the road. If they were in any place for more than a day, I was going to try to be there. At least that gave us a little hope, which is all we had to go on. I still believed that I should tell Biff, but Willie asked me to wait until we could work some things out first. So I told him I would. I dreaded facing Biff when I got home because I felt that guilt was written all over my face. But when he picked me up at the airport in Los Angeles, I guess it wasn't.

He was so happy to see me that it made me feel terrible. Like I said, I'd never lied to him since we'd been married. He told me he had missed me, our dog Rusty had missed me, and asked if I had a good time and how the show was. I answered everything except for the question on how the show was; I sort of skirted around it. He must have felt the answer was all right and then he asked me if I'd brought back Willie's check, which I had done. Willie had signed a check for $1,000 but it wouldn't be any good because he didn't have any money yet. So I was trying to find a way to keep Biff from taking the check and depositing it. I made some feeble excuse that we needed to hold the check until Willie called. I was relieved when he said we would hold onto it. Biff was always all business, especially about money. After that, were few questions about Atlanta, and I certainly didn't offer any other information. Biff really had no reason to be suspicious of anything. At this point, I felt that I was leading two different lives;

being unfaithful and lying to the man I was married to, and waiting for the man I loved to call.

Willie called every day. He figured out that the time when Biff was on the air and he would call. Sometimes I'd hear the background noise of cars and trucks, and I'd know he was calling at some pay phone off the Interstate somewhere. Other times he would only get to say "I love you" and then the operator would say "more money please," but the fact that he was calling meant the world to me. I wonder now how I hid those calls from Biff because they always made me feel good. Then the day came when he called and said Ray was going to be in Oklahoma City for two days and then he'd be going to Houston and wondered if I would try to make Oklahoma City. I didn't know what excuse to use this time, other than the one I'd used before. So again, I told Biff that Ray wanted me to sing for him again in Oklahoma City.

This was really quite an honor, so Biff said that I could hardly refuse. Television was winding down for me and my records were still doing well. By the late 1950s, I was the number-three Country singer in the nation. I continued to guest on the "Town Hall Party" and other country television shows, but nothing steady like "Country America" had been. So the chance to sing for Ray Price was a good deal. I felt like the time to leave would never come. I arranged to be in Oklahoma City a day in advance to surprise Willie. I decided to stay in the penthouse of the hotel I was in. It was absolutely beautiful and I thought it would be great fun for both of us. As much as I traveled on the road, I'd never stayed in the Penthouse of any hotel I had stayed in. It had a fireplace and came with champagne; the whole works. I could afford to stay anyplace I wanted. If you remember Biff let me keep the money I made working in my own account. He didn't take any of it and I had quite a bit saved up. So we were going to stay there in style.

When Willie called I told him to come on to the hotel, and was he ever surprised. He walked around in the rooms and looked at everything. We had a wonderful view of the city too. He wanted to know if it would be all right with me if he invited Jimmy Day to come up and eat supper with us. I told him it would be fine and we called Jimmy and arranged to meet him in the lobby. He didn't tell him we were in the Penthouse, but when they got off the elevator, Jimmy went nuts. He said, "This is a blast!" Ray's bass player was in the Penthouse and Ray was sleeping on the bus. Funny, isn't it?

I don't have to say how excited that Willie and I were together again. Once again, we're already trying to figure out how to be together longer and we've just seen one another for the second time. We were so in love that it was pitiful, but beautiful. For the next two days, we just enjoyed doing nothing but being relaxed and living like we were rich.

When the time came to leave each other, Willie said he had an idea that I should go on to Houston with him and the band. I didn't think I should be riding around on the bus, so we did the only sensible thing: we chartered a plane. Now that's thinking for you. From Houston, Ray and the band would be going back to Nashville, so we'd just take the plane to Texas and then back to Oklahoma City. That way, we'd have an extra day or so together. So that's what we did. Not only did Ray have a bass man that stayed in the Penthouse, but he now chartered a plane to his next job. I mean the band really teased him about it and by now they were all beginning to know what was going on between Willie and me.

No one said anything to us about what was going on, not even Ray. I guess maybe they felt it would be better to stay neutral in a matter like this. But this time, Biff would track me down. After I didn't come back from Oklahoma City when I should have, he found out where Ray was playing and he called me. It just happened that I sat in with them and that I was singing, so I guess when the club owner told him I was singing, he didn't know what to say. What he did say was "why didn't you come home or call?" Then he said, "Do you want to tell me what's going on?"

By this time, I knew that when I did get back to California, no matter what Willie said, I was going to tell him. And that's exactly what I did when I got home. I planted my feet firmly in the living room carpet and told Biff that I didn't love him anymore. I was in love with Willie and we wanted to be together. He said the only thing he could say, "You're crazy!" He meant it too. I tried to reason with him that I wasn't crazy. He told me everything bad that he could think of about Willie; that he was no good and he'd never amount to anything. At the time, I was wondering about all the good things he had said about him a couple of months ago. Then Biff called our doctor and had him come over to see us. I told him the same thing. I was in love with Willie Nelson, and I didn't want to stay with Biff any longer.

He told Biff what he thought had happened, and this I'll never forget, "Willie and Shirley are on the same wave length and no matter what you say, she isn't going to change her mind. At least not now! Just be patient and things will change."

The one thing that did change was the phone number. But that wouldn't stop me. I would get the phone number to someone who would get it to Willie. You know, many times when people to fall in love, other people will help you to be together if they can. We did have a few friends.

On one of those conversations with Willie, he knew by now that Biff knew about us. He told me he was coming back to California to record for Joe and he was going to take me away with him. Biff had taken the coil or something off of my car so, unless I wanted to walk, I wasn't going anywhere without him. He took time off from work and he wanted us to go away together for a little while. But the end result was that I wouldn't go. Our household was not too civilized at this time. I don't mean I was mean to him, I just wouldn't talk to him. Biff talked about what we had together and what a good life we could continue to have together, but all I could think about was that Willie was coming back to California and I'd be seeing him somehow.

But when he did come out, I didn't get to see him. He was just there a few days and he had to fly back to Nashville. We did talk he told me that I was going to be recording again in Nashville and that maybe I should try to regain Biff's confidence again so I could make it. Willie always seemed to know when I was going to record and this time would be extra special because Joe had decided that Willie and I should record together. I don't believe Biff wanted too many people to know about Willie and me, so when Joe called and said that I needed to come to Nashville to record, Biff didn't make any excuses why I shouldn't.

By this time, I was trying not to act so hateful and was hoping that before long Biff would try to understand my feelings. I really wasn't ready to leave with Willie because we actually didn't have any place to go, not yet, anyway. So I had to be, as they say now, cool. I was probably the most uncool person anyone ever met. Biff took me to the airport. For some reason he couldn't go with me—maybe because of work, I'm not sure. He said he'd be calling me every night I was gone, and that he loved me and he hoped I'd give up on this silly infatuation I had for Willie.

I didn't say yes or no. I said something like, "We'll just have to wait and see, and we'll talk about it when I get back." I thought when I did get back I would be moving out and getting a divorce. But Biff's vocabulary had no such word as divorce. He had been married once before, to Floyd Tillman's ex-wife, Marge, and he certainly didn't want to go through that again. In fact, the song "Slipping Around" that Floyd wrote was about Biff and Marge. Biff made the comparison several times. He had taken a songwriter's wife away and now a songwriter was taking his wife away. What in the world was going to happen to us? That's all I thought about on the plane to Nashville. What were we going to do?

I went right to my hotel when I arrived. I was really exhausted from all these troubles I was having. I thought I'd just rest and wait for Joe to call with the recording time for me. He called and asked me if I felt like coming up to his hotel for a little bit. He said he thought he had a great idea. I guess I felt that if I got out for a while maybe I would feel better. Biff had already called to see if I made it all right and to see how I was. When I got up to Joe's room, who did I see sitting on the floor with a guitar, but Willie! Willie and I were going to record. Joe had plans for the first man and woman duet and it would be Willie and me.

He wanted to hear how we sounded together and we sounded like we'd always sung together. Willie said later that he thought I seconded guessed him when we sang, but I think, as the doctor said, "we were on the same wave length."

Now Joe Allison was an old friend of Biff's, so Willie and I didn't do anything out of the ordinary. Hank Cochran was there too and he had a song he wanted us to do, if Joe would agree. The song was "Willingly." The first words I would sing were "Willingly I fell in love with you." Then Willie would sing, "Willingly I learned to love you too." Our duet would go on to become Willie's first top-ten record and a big seller. The words said everything we wanted to say to each other. After people knew that Willie and I were together, they thought he had written it, but it was Hank Cochran's song.

While we were in the room, Willie presented a song to Joe for the other side of the record called "Chain of Love." Later when I read reviews of this duet, the critics said I performed vocal gymnastics. When I listened to it, I guess I felt that they were right. It's very difficult to figure out who's singing harmony and who's singing the lead. Our voices blended so well it was like magic. Joe thought so too!

Willie walked me back to my hotel and then we agreed it would be better if we didn't see too much of each other while I was there. We held hands and my heart ached, but I knew it had to be that way. While I didn't ask him how his divorce was coming along, I did tell him what I intended to do when I got back to California. He told me again that "because we loved each other so much, things will work out." I believed him with all my heart.

The next morning, by ten o'clock, we would be singing "Willingly" and, if that wasn't a premonition of what was going to happen, nothing was. After we finished the session, I had a tape made so I could listen when I got back home. It was beautiful. The last thing Willie said to me was that we've got to make Biff see how serious this is between the two of us, and by the time I got back home, another plan was taking form.

When Biff listened to the tape, he asked me where I had learned to sign like that. He played it over and over and was surprised that Willie and I had recorded together. I told him it wasn't my idea, but that it was Joe's. He probably checked it out. I'm not sure. I think he knew at that time how much I was in love with Willie, but he didn't say. What he did say was that he felt I should undergo some psychological testing in order to save our marriage, because he thought I wasn't acting normal. I agreed to go for a few tests, and they found out that I was as normal as could be. But it they would have known what I was about to do, they might have had different thoughts.

Willie got through to me on the phone and told me that Ray was going to Canada for 30 days. He thought I should meet them in Seattle, Washington and go with him. This was bound to show everyone how serious we were. There'd be no going back to California after that! So I began to plan how I was going to do it. By this time, I'm trying to act like I've forgotten about Willie, so Biff put the coil back on the car that he had taken off earlier. Then I was able to go where I wanted to. I knew I had to fly, so I had to figure out how to get a flight and my ticket without Biff knowing. I didn't know how I was going to work things out.

I called a travel bureau and had them look at direct flights to Seattle. As luck would have it, I got my wish. I withdrew some cash out of my bank account and bought my ticket from the travel agency. Then I waited for the day I would be leaving.

In about two or three days, Biff went to work and, by the afternoon, I was at the Los Angeles airport waiting for my plane and watching the clock. But of course, the plane was running late. If Biff got home before I left, I knew the first place he'd look was at the airport. So I kept hoping that the plane would hurry up and leave, which it finally did. I was so relieved to in the air at last, and headed toward Seattle and Willie.

When we landed, Willie and Jimmy Day were waiting for me at my arrival gate. What a beautiful sight they were. I really had suffered the whole trip wondering if at any minute someone would come back to my seat and tell me that Mr. Collie had arranged for the authorities to pick me up and take me back home. I did plan on calling him at some point, and telling him that the car was at the airport in Los Angeles. I figured when we got ready to go into Canada, I'd do just that. But for this moment, I was just glad to be back in Willie's arms. We hadn't been together for a while and with him just holding me, everything seemed to be all right.

We went on to the hotel, all of us arm-in-arm. When we got there, Willie told me he had asked Ray about me going with them and that he had agreed to let me; he'd take care of me. Can you imagine what thoughts were going through my head before I fell asleep that night? I'd run away from everything I was so sure that I would've kept forever; Biff, my career, my friends, and my family. No one knew where I was or if I was all right. I figured they might start looking the next day, or maybe they were already looking. I wished we were already in Canada, and in a way, I truly wished that it hadn't have led me to "running away."

One thing I did learn was that when you tell someone who loves you the truth, like I did, that it might have been better if I hadn't. But here I was with Willie, and before the month was over, there would be many changes in store for me. As my life had changed at 14, when I left home to work in radio, then again at 20 when I went to Texas and back into television with Red Foley, then again to the Philip Morris show and Biff, this would be the biggest change of all. I had let myself be captured by a redheaded bass player and songwriter.

The next morning, after breakfast, we walked around and Willie took me to the jewelry shop next door to the hotel. He wanted to buy me a ring. I had gotten him a blue sapphire ring, sometime back, and he loved it. Now he wanted to buy me a ring. We looked in the window and, at the same time, we both saw a wide gold wedding band. I looked at Willie and sort of laughed and said, "You do want to marry me don't you?"

He said, "You know I do, so let's get the ring." He had some engraving done on it and when we picked it up later in the afternoon, I looked inside of the band and read, "I promise you love, forever and after forever. Your Willie."

I took off the silver band Biff Collie had given me and Willie put the gold band on my finger. The only problem was that he was still married and I was still married. But we were both running away to Canada and we were happy. Incredible! Imagine Shirley Caddell Collie and honorary Cherokee Cowboy. Super!!!

Why leave home? Why did I leave? It wasn't for the security of being with Willie, because I knew he wasn't being paid all that much money to be a front man. It wasn't for a different career. At this time, I had no idea what I'd be doing in a year. Hopefully, we'd be somewhere together. It wasn't for the excitement. My life wasn't in a rut. I had television to do, personal appearances, recording, and, supposedly, a part on the "Beverly Hillbillies," if I'd stay.

The answer that I keep coming up with was I left home for total devotion and love. In my eyes, this man was simply great! I'd have the chance to watch him perform, to sing and play, and I saw the way the audiences reacted to him. I'm just not sure if at the time he saw it. Anyway, I was with him and that was all that mattered. Finding the reason and self-analysis would come much later.

I felt sure Biff had to know where I was, but he told other people that he didn't. He called my mom and dad in Missouri, and upset them terribly. I don't know exactly what he said, but Mom told me later that he was trying to act like maybe I'd gotten amnesia or I had been kidnapped. Again, I don't know what he told his radio listeners either. It was traumatic for him, too, as I look at it now. Don't let me mislead you; I wasn't going around with my head in the clouds. I had anxiety attacks on the bus; I couldn't breathe, at least that's how I felt. I also had terrible guilt feelings at different times, but never once did I feel like turning back. I knew that someday, I'd have to see Biff again. But I would rather it had been sooner than later and then everything would be over. But I also could see that it wasn't going to be that way for me. There were lots of bad feelings involved and many people involved as well.

I'm not leaving out Martha or the children either. How would they react when they found out about me? That Cherokee Indian temper might go on the warpath. I just really didn't want to fight with anyone, but I would if I had to. I knew all these questions were going around in Willie's mind too. In fact, many years later I found out that he called Joe Allison, our Liberty producer, and asked him, "Aren't you and Biff Collie good friends?"

Joe, of course, answered, "Yes."

Willie said, "Well, I'm going to give you the chance to fire me off the record label before we get started." Of course, Joe was startled and asked him why he said that.

Willie replied, "I'm going to run away with his wife!"

At this point, Joe told me that he said he wasn't going to get involved with any personal feeling in this, and that it wasn't his problem and that he wanted Willie to stay on the label. Joe thought I had heard this conversation, but I hadn't. It made me feel proud of the man I loved. He was also willing to sacrifice his career for what he believed in, love. If you've never had these feelings, I only hope that someday you can experience them. I know I've said this before, but I'm going to keep saying it; no one had ever loved me the way he did.

As we traveled across Canada, it seemed to get colder and colder. One morning when the bus had stopped for us to eat, I asked them to let me sleep and someone told me to wake up and start knitting because it was 56 degrees below zero. That was the actual temperature. I neglected to tell you that I didn't take along my knitting. The practical side of me would have been knitting those sock-shoes to keep our feet warm. But this was serious business. I had to get going on them before everyone's feet were frozen. I said I'd need to get some more yarn when we stopped for the night and, while everyone was doing the show, I went shopping.

Faron Young had joined the show for a few days and he wanted gray socks, and everyone wanted different colors. So that kept me busy for a while. Faron had just recorded Willie's "Hello Walls" and Faron was going to have a big big record. He was with us just a little while and I got his socks finished so he could take them with him. He said he'd see us in Toronto later.

This adjusting to the cold weather kind of got the better of me, and by the time we got to Toronto, I had strep throat. Willie called the doctor from the hotel, and he came and gave me some shots and said that I had to stay in bed.

Ray was going to work out of Toronto for the next few days and when they were ready to leave for their show, Willie wouldn't go with them. He told Ray that I was too sick to be left alone and that I was bordering on laryngitis, and that I wouldn't be able to call anyone if I needed something. I'm not sure how Ray took that, but he didn't fire Willie. So I suppose he just went along with it. Anyway, he was sitting there in the room with me and the phone rang. Naturally, he answered and I couldn't believe what I heard. He was talking to my mother in Chillicothe, Missouri.

She had tracked us down and ended up calling Canada to see if I was all right. To this day, she's never told me how she did that. I suspect Biff had some input, but she wouldn't say. Willie reassured her that I had a sore throat and that he was taking care of me and we'd been with the doctor and that everything was fine. I don't know much more about the conversation, except that it seemed to be going along on an even keel.

Willie seemed to explain things pretty well to Mom. That, in itself, was a miracle. She said that she'd see us when we get back and Willie hung up the phone and looked at me and laughed telling me that it was, "your mother." I remember that I had a really bad night. I was sort of prone to sore throats and after all I had put myself through the last few months, I was probably exhausted, too. But within the next couple of days, I began to get better, but I ended up not being able to talk.

I want to tell you a very funny story about not being able to talk. Faron Young and I did not have a close relationship. He and I had been on quite a few shows together over the years. The one thing I found very unattractive about Faron, as everyone knows, was his bad language. Now I was not so goody goody that I'd never heard bad talk before. But I felt if I would just leave when he came in, I wouldn't have to listen to him. Anyway, he happened to be back stage in one of the dressing rooms, in Toronto, where I was waiting for Willie to finish his show with Ray. Remember, I couldn't talk because of my throat, so Faron proceeded to tell me not only was I a snob, but I was also the most stuck-up person he'd ever met. He said just awhile back on TV in California, that he came into the make-up room and I looked at him and went out the other door. What in the hell was my problem? I just looked at him and remained sitting down. He kept trying to get me to fuss with him, but if you look at the way I did, it was kind of funny. Finally, he gave up and left the room, mumbling something under his breath.

Later that night, when Willie and I were in our room, he wanted to know what happened when Faron was in the dressing room. I wasn't going to tell him, but he seemed upset over it for some reason, so I did. He jumped up and told me he was going up to his room and whip up on him. I tried to calm him down, but he was really mad that Faron had talked to me that way. Willie didn't see any humor in it, either. Anyway, he went to find Faron. I knew Faron had a temper and I just saw Willie have one, so I didn't know what was going to happen. I just sat there and waited.

In a little bit, he came back and told me that Faron would like to apologize to me the next day. Willie said that I should have taken back his knitted shoes I made for him. I told him we should just forget it. Faron and I went on to be great friends, but I did get my apology the next day.

We kept moving on across Canada and I got to see some lovely country. What amazed me the most about the Canadian people who came to the show was that there might not be a soul there before showtime, and then all of a sudden there were people all over the place. They loved Ray's music too. Of course, everyone loved Ray and the Cherokee Cowboys. They were one of the top acts. At this time, everyone's bus boy, Ben Dorsey, was with them on the bus. He kind of did all the odd chores for the guys, and he did lots of things for Ray. He carried instruments in and helped unload the bus.

On this particular night they were playing a theater and Ray was really going over big. He came off stage and laid his guitar down on the case, and then he went back on stage again to wave to the crowd. They wanted more music. When he came back to get his guitar, it was gone. Ray was having a fit. He wanted to know, in no uncertain terms, where his guitar was. The crowd was roaring and Ben told him that he'd already packed it away. In the space of a minute or two it was gone. But in the space of another minute or two, it was back. All of the band members were laughing like crazy. But that's the way Ben did things.

Shortly after that, in the middle of the night, Ray put Ben off the bus in the middle of nowhere. Ray thought Ben had been stealing money from the band members. But Ben was waiting for the bus when we pulled into Nashville back home. How he did that I'll never know. I would probably have sat down and froze to death.

The days were moving along pretty fast, and I knew everything was going to change shortly after we got back. Willie and I had begun to have discussions about what we should and should not do. He had already said that he was going to have Ray stop the bus in Goodlettsville, Tennessee and he was going to go get his car. That sounded pretty good, but I really was a little doubtful that Martha was going to give him the car for us to run around in. I knew I should call Biff and proceed with a divorce. I needed to get some more money from California and call my folks in Missouri. Then as we were moving across Canada, I had two job offers.

One came from Helen Carter, and the other came from Ray Price. Helen's husband, Glenn Jones, was Ray Price's bus driver at the time. Helen Carter, of the very famous Carter Family, had been booked to do some shows in Canada with Ray. We got to talking, which Helen and I loved to do, and she asked me if I might be interested in becoming a member of the Carter Family—she meant a singing member of the family. She and Anita needed someone to help out on the harmony when she, June, and Anita were singing. I felt so honored to be asked, but like I told her, I really didn't know what Willie and I were planning to do yet. But I did promise to keep in touch with her.

I'm one of the few people who knew the original words to "Wildwood Flower" and I've always been a fan of the Carters. It seems funny, but Helen and I would talk again almost thirty years to the day, and we'd be talking about the same things. Only this time I was asking her if she needed me. Are we in the twilight zone or what? Seems just like yesterday!

The other offer would come from Ray Price. Willie had already told Ray when we got back to the United States that he was leaving. Well, I guess that settled that! Ray wanted me to try and convince Willie to stay on as bass player and front man, and he would hire me as a girl singer for his band. I'll tell you that that, too, was an honor – just to be asked. But I told him no. Willie and I, by this time, had talked and we both knew that we were going to rest up just a bit and then get me a divorce. The uppermost thing in our minds was to stay together.

Willie felt that Martha knew about us for sure, and he was certain that she'd go ahead with their divorce. We thought we'd probably have some trouble with Biff, but if we kind of got our bearings, we'd be able to handle anything. When we came back into the United States and on through to Tennessee, the temperature wasn't all that high. But anything above 20 degrees felt like summer after the cold we had in Canada.

I will never forget the day when we left Ray's bus. Glenn stopped almost right across from Willie's house in Goodlettsville. We unloaded our suitcases and instruments. Little Guitar had been along with me all through this trip. I wouldn't have thought about leaving her, and Willie had fallen completely in love with her. I stood by the side of the highway, probably looking like something or someone out of a bad movie. It seems, if I remember right, that it was about mid morning and the bus drove away. I looked over at Willie's house and saw these little children playing in the yard. They weren't very old and when they saw Willie, they started yelling.

It made me feel bad that he was going in just to get the car and then come back for me. You could see that the kids were crazy about him. It seemed like I stood there forever. It really wasn't very long though, because in just a little while Willie came running back to me, minus the car. It was a wonder that Martha wasn't running after him with the broom or something more lethal, but she wasn't. I don't know if she knew I was even standing on the roadway waiting and wondering if everything we talked about in Canada was really going to happen, but here he was.

He told me that we'd have to catch a ride on in to town and then we'd get a cab and go on downtown and check into a hotel somewhere. Believe it or not, I was completely exhausted from the stress. All I wanted to do was to get someplace and sit down and that's just what we did. I don't remember who picked us up, but someone must have taken pity on us and before I knew it, we were in downtown Nashville at the Downtowner Motor Hotel across from the WSM Studios.

I had stayed there once or twice when I'd come in to record. We had a small suite and, like I said, I just wanted to lay down and rest for a while. I laid down and Willie covered me up with a blanket and told me that he had several things he needed to attend to, and he'd be back before I woke up. He told me not to worry and I knew everything was going to turn out all right. I guess he wanted to go back out to his publisher Pamper Music in Goodlettsville and see Hal Smith to find out how things were going for him money wise. I understood what he was doing so just relaxed and fell asleep.

As soon as all of our friends found out we were back in Nashville, we had one continuous open house. People were coming in and going out almost all of the time. I called to California and had the rest of my money sent from the bank. Willie found out that he'd be getting a pretty good sized royalty check in a couple of weeks, so we were fixed pretty good. I didn't hear from Biff, except in a round-a-bout way.

I called Mom and told her more about Willie. She told me that Biff had called again, but she didn't tell him she'd talked to Willie and me, or where we were. Sneaky little critter, wasn't she? I feel sure that he knew anyway. I didn't really know what Dad's feelings were about all this, and she didn't say. I'd say he was just going to let me make my own mistakes. At this particular time, in our lives, we were so caught up in each other that I believe, at times, we were not really in the real world. I say this because I know now there was a lot of people who didn't like Willie and me being together. I think that, had they known all the circumstances, people would have had different thoughts. But you know the good outweighs the bad.

What I'm getting at is that we still had lots of friends to surround and support us. Almost all of our entertainer and songwriter friends, like Patsy Kline and Hank Cochran, to name a few, came to see us while we were in town. I guess we were an unlikely pair, at least for the moment anyway. I had always been so straight and narrow, never faltering from what I was doing. Then to run off helter skelter was crazy. I was running off with a sideman who was only being paid week to week and he had a family. One thing for sure is that we weren't hiding from anyone. There we were right in the middle of downtown Nashville.

I had occasion to see Ralph Emery of "Nashville Now" fame about thirty years later and he said, "Do you remember the last time I saw you?" I couldn't but he told me it was in the motel across from WSM where he had his all-night radio show. We really left a lasting impression with him. But time was moving on and we needed to get on with our life. We decided that as soon as the money was available we would go to Reno, Nevada and get me a divorce. It only took six weeks and everything would be over. Wishful thinking on our part as I look at it now.

I had to go out there and establish residence and then file. We knew it would be expensive, but that's what we were going to do. So early one morning, when all was ready, we rented a car and off we went to Reno. I've got to tell you that was a trip to remember. If two people ever got to know each other, we did. We'd been all over Canada together, but you don't truly get to know each other until you're locked up in a car together like we were. If you ever want to know someone, try it, it works. By the time you get where you're going, I guarantee you that you'll either love them more or your won't be able to stand each other.

As it was, our trip turned out to be more love, at times, than not. I say at times because at other times we argued then we'd stop and make up. The make-up part was great. It took us two weeks to get from Nashville to Reno, and it was the best trip I ever had in my life. I'd just like to tell you, at this time, why it took us so long. It was a bit unusual.

We began talking about everyday stuff, such as what a person should or shouldn't do. You must remember that I'd just come from being an established person so at the moment I was set in my ways. Anyhow, I felt you should do things by the book and Willie felt differently. If he had a change of clothes, he said fine and he'd buy some more when he ran out. I thought you needed a different outfit for each day. He was not, or had not been, affected by rational things. He didn't believe you should pay income tax, have a driver's license, or be any of the card-carrying people in this world. He didn't have a social security number and I was really annoyed about that. I'd had one forever.

I remembered my mom back in Chillicothe taking me to get my card years and years ago. The folks let me work in summer washing dishes in a little café and I had to get my social security card. Anyway, that was just a few of the things that went wrong on the trip. Over a matter of days, we went on and on about all the things you should have and do. Like I said, we would discuss and argue and then we'd stop, check in to a hotel, eat supper, and be in love again before we started out the next morning.

I don't remember exactly how we went out there, but we did see some beautiful scenery. We would stop and get out of the car and look around. It was wonderful, sort of like a cross-country vacation. Neither one of us had really ever had a vacation like that before. The nearest I had had was Biff and I going to Texas or Missouri when he had his vacation time off and, believe it or not, he always planned it to be an experiment of some kind. Like the time we went to San Antonio in his new Renault, a very small car, with our Myna bird, Woodles, in the back seat, and no air conditioning. I believe that this was a true test on nerves. When it got too hot to believe, Woodles had to have cold towels put around her cage to just keep on living. I laugh now, but I didn't then. I believe it was an experiment on how much gas the Renault could save and how much I could stand Woodles. Funny?

Anyway, back to Willie and me. I tried to explain to him that in this world there were certain things a person had to do and, above all, it was very important that he paid his income tax. He laughed and told me, "Up to now, I haven't had any income." But I assured him that, with his songs, he would have an income before long and people would be watching him and making inquiries.

So, anyway, we had time to get all these things straightened out after we got through with Reno. So forward we went with just the three of us, Willie, me, and "Baby," the Little Martin. We found a nice furnished apartment not far from downtown. Then we began to make inquiries about a lawyer. We found a good one and in just six weeks, I'd be free, or so I thought. After all the papers were filed, and since I wasn't asking Biff for anything, it seemed to be relatively simple. But in the end, it turned out not to be.

After Biff got my papers from Nevada, he cross-filed in California and the divorce from him would not be granted for one year. I had to go on with the divorce in Reno and, in fact, I would still be divorced in six weeks, but not totally or completely free until a year later. But Willie and I decided that we could handle that all right; together we could lick the world. I didn't care what anybody thought of me. Our love would last much longer than their thoughts of me. I wanted Willie and I needed his love, that's all I knew. I loved him and I'd forgive the world before I'd ever let him go.

I'd fight the World
I don't care what anybody thinks of me
Our love would last much longer than their thoughts of me
I want you and I need your love
That's all I know
And I'd fight the world before I'd ever let you go.

Believe it or not, we did have a good time while we were in Reno. We started going to some casino shows and meeting people, mostly musicians we knew, and Willie was already among the entertainers becoming well-known. Another thing we liked to do was grocery shopping. We were both like little kids. Willie would just throw anything in the cart so I had to really watch him. He enrolled in a gym and started working out with a boxer, but after I saw the way his face was punched around, I wanted him to quit. But he didn't. We played Little Guitar, wrote songs, sang together and, at night, studied the Bible. Willie would read verse after verse and then we'd talk about what we'd read. It was wonderful just being together.

But all things for me had to change, as you know, and after the divorce in Reno, I had the worst case of guilt feelings that I've ever had. I felt bad because Willie wasn't with his kids and because I hadn't faced up to Biff before I ran off to Canada. I just really felt bad about everything. I had to do something about it, even if it meant leaving Willie for a few days. I had to go back to San Gabriel and make everything final. Willie and I talked about it and that's what I did. But the circumstances turned out to be terrible and before I could get back to Willie, a whole lot of trouble would come about.

Remember true love never runs smooth and we were in for a rough battle. Willie decided that he would go to Fort Worth where his sister, Bobbie, and her family lived. There he would wait until I could come to him. We figured it would only be a matter of a week or so.

We'd talked to Bobbie on the phone from Reno and she was anxious to meet me. I already knew I was going to love her like a sister, which I still do today and always will. Anyway, I knew I was welcome there and I knew Willie would be all right until I could get back to him.

I'm not saying going back to California was a good idea. It just seemed to me to be the right thing to do. I did have a few things in our house there that I thought I would like to have. Remember, when I went to Canada I only took my guitar and one suitcase. That's probably the lightest I've ever traveled in my entire life. Anyway, we got things straightened out in Reno. We gave up the apartment and Willie would catch a plane to Texas and I'd be driving to San Gabriel. If I had known what was about to happen, I would never have gone. It wasn't too long of a drive, as I remember. It gave me a chance to organize my thoughts and to work out what I had to say to Biff. Most of all, I hated leaving Willie. It felt like part of me was gone. We'd been together night and day for several months and the leaving was hard to do.

When I got to San Gabriel it was early evening and Biff was working on his show at his typewriter. I knocked on the door and he opened it. He didn't speak; he just sat down in the chair and looked at me. It was the kind of look from him I'd never seen before. All I can say is that is sure was strange. I really believe he thought I'd lost my mind. I told him I needed to talk to him. I had no intention of staying any longer that I had to, and still he just stared at me.

He didn't appear to be angry because I knew he had a bad temper when he was mad. He didn't even look hurt. Now I believe he looked like he had a plan, which he certainly did have—a big plan for me.

Finally, when he did speak, he talked to me like I was a child. He asked if he could get me something to eat or drink, was I tired, did I feel all right; these were some of his questions. He brought Rusty, my peke, into the living room and told me how much he and the dog had missed me. Then he asked me if I didn't want to rest for a while. He would go up to Aunt Mary's house, which was just across the backyard, and stay and I could have the house to myself. I didn't argue with him and I knew that if he went up there I would call Fort Worth and see if Willie made it to Bobbie's house all right. You see, even through going back to see Biff again, all I wanted was to be with Willie.

He was still uppermost in my mind. Biff gathered a few things together, gave Aunt Mary a call, and told me he'd see me before he went to work. I guess I really was exhausted, so I just lay down on the couch with my clothes on, with Rusty lying on my feet, and fell asleep. In about an hour I woke up and decided I'd better call Texas and let Willie know how things were going so far.

It was good to hear his voice. In fact, he answered the phone as soon as it rang. Bobbie told me, when I talked to her later, that Willie had been sitting by the phone waiting on my call. I told Willie that I loved him and couldn't wait until we were back together. He said that on the plane to Texas he's made a few decisions about what we should do and we'd talk them over when I got there. I hated to hang up, but I knew I needed to rest, as I was mentally and physically worn out. But I told him that I'd call him the minute I left.

I had intended to fly so he'd be meeting me at the airport in just a few days. I also told Willie I'd give him a call in the morning after Biff left, and he said he'd be waiting. The last thing Willie said to me was "Don't ever forget how much I love you." Before I went to sleep, I wondered if Biff knew I'd called Willie or if he thought I'd be leaving again in the middle of the night. But I wasn't going anywhere until Biff and I had the chance to talk this out. At least that's what I thought. But how wrong we sometimes are.

The next morning, Biff did not come by soon enough to talk. He told me he would arrange to take off the following day and then we could get everything settled. I began to gather up what I wanted to take with me. Not too much, just my clothes and personal things I'd left behind. Along about noon the phone rang and I answered it. The voice on the other end said, "Hello, is this Mrs. Collie? This is Happy

Valley Acres," or some such place, I don't remember just now. She wanted to know how old I was.

I decided immediately that I'd better go along with this and find out what was going on. I told her what she wanted to know and then she said we're expecting you tomorrow by four o'clock. I was really shocked, but I tried not to show it in my voice. I was being committed to a fancy funny farm and if I didn't do something quick, I was on my way. I asked her if I could bring my guitar and she said, "Of course, we'd love to have you play." I hung up, knowing I was going to have to do something right that minute. In California, a husband, and Biff was still my husband, could put you away like that and it's legal if they fear for your safety or if they think you're out of your mind, which is exactly what he thought.

Anyway, I called immediately to Fort Worth for Willie. I told him what Biff was planning and if we didn't do something he'd probably never see me again. Biff would rather have me crazy than with Willie. He told me to just hang on and he'd be here as soon as he could get a car. And get a car is just what he did.

Bobbie's husband, Paul, ran a used car lot and he let Willie borrow a car. I don't know if he even put the right license on it; he told me that he was stopped so many times that he couldn't count them. Finally he took off and had Bobbie call and tell me he was on his way. When he crossed into California, he would call and tell me to get out of the house and meet him somewhere. That must have been the wildest ride anyone ever took, from Fort Worth, Texas to San Gabriel, California. I don't know exactly how many miles that is, but I'm sure he set some kind of a record on time. He was stopped at the state line for not having any registration and he had to call back to Texas and verify that everything was all right.

My sweet, sweet love was coming after me, and I was going to be safe with him at last. It seemed like an eternity until he finally called. All I was waiting for was that call, and when he did call it was going to be bye-bye California and Biff Collie, and hello Texas or wherever we could just be together and get away from trouble. I left some kind of note on the door that said I'd gone to get a dress for the television show and I'd be back a little later. Many years later Biff told about the note and that was the longest time he had ever waited for anyone to come home.

So I took my clothes and my guitars and left the car in front of the drug store in San Gabriel, and Willie and I took off for the border. I had never in my life been so happy to see him and I promised myself that if I were with him, nothing was going to ever part us again.

When we made it into Arizona and finally stopped, we held each other for the longest time. I truly believed that Willie had made the same promise, too. We phoned back to Biff, who was home by this time, and finally said goodbye. I told him if he wanted to, I would be sending him an address later where the rest of my things could be sent. I believe he finally realized that we were serious. I was anxious to get on to Fort Worth to see Bobbie. As I said, I'd talked to her on the phone but I was finally going to be meeting her and her family.

When we got to Bobbie's I believe I slept for two or three days, I was so worn out. One funny episode happened during our sleeping time there. Bobbie's youngest son, Freddy, sensed he had some pretty important company in the middle bedroom. I remember waking up and I thought I saw these little kids coming by the bed. But surely I was dreaming, so I just went back to sleep. When we finally did get up, I asked Bobbie if anything strange had been going on. She laughed and said that Freddy had been charging the neighbor kids a nickel to look at Uncle Willie and Aunt Shirley, and he had a pretty good business going until she put a stop to it. So much for our small businessman. He's never forgotten that incident, either. We still laugh about it.

It was really difficult to believe that after all the trouble we'd been through that Willie and I were together at last. For a while, after getting to Fort Worth, I couldn't stop thinking that something else might happen that would tear us apart. For the most part, we just enjoyed being together with Bobbie, Paul and their family, going out to eat, riding around in the car, and just being together and in love.

[Counter clockwise: Willie, me, Bobbie, unknown, Paul, and Tommy Alsup]

I knew Willie was missing his kids, but I wouldn't ask why he didn't call them until we'd been together for probably two or three weeks. I guess I was shocked when he told me that Martha had moved them and he didn't know where they were. I couldn't believe what I was hearing. We had to do something to find them. I know he made lots of calls. They were supposed to be in Las Vegas with Martha, but it turned out that they weren't. He said all he knew was to call their grandparents in Waco. When he did, we found out that they were there. What a wonderful surprise to find that they were only a few miles from us.

I know I was finally saying "us" and "we," and believe me when I say that I wanted everything and everyone in his life to be part of mine. My whole world was Willie Nelson. The only thing out of my world that had come with me was my Little Martin. Willie adored her and he gave her the name "Baby." I left my world behind and looked to something brand new with him. Today, as I write those lines, it seems so unreal that I would do the things I did. Completely secure in the knowledge that I was losing in my money, home, and family. I gave them all away for the love of a good man, with no thought of what could or would happen.

Fate does deal us strange hands sometimes, as I would find out in later years. But at that time, again, I say that my world was Willie. It didn't matter to me whether or not I had anything as long as I was with him. Willie had a way of letting you know that he'd take care of you, no matter what.

We had found the kids and we were going to Waco to see them. I had seen them from a distance when he left Ray Price back there when I was waiting by the side of the road for him to come get me. But when I finally did see them up close, they were truly adorable.

We got to Paul and Nanny's, Martha's folks, house and Lana, the oldest, was in the yard playing in the plastic swimming pool. It was the kind of pool you would buy in a Wal-Mart store. She was a lovely little dark complexion girl, very Indian looking, splashing around and having a good time. Billy looked like a little Indian too, but Susie was a picture of blonde curls and light skin like her Aunt Bobbie. With Martha, of course being a Cherokee Indian, the kids would naturally have some of her genes. I loved them immediately.

They were running around in their bathing suits wanting to love their Daddy. They had missed him so much. But now everybody would be together again, at least for a little while. Willie talked to Nanny and she told him that Martha had left them but they'd be going back to Las Vegas in a couple of months. Willie left Nanny some money for all of them and she promised that she'd let him know where they always would be, until he could get things straightened out with Martha. We left Waco to go back to Fort Worth and I think he was feeling a little better because he'd been with his kids. But I hoped that before long, they'd be with us for his sake, and mine too.

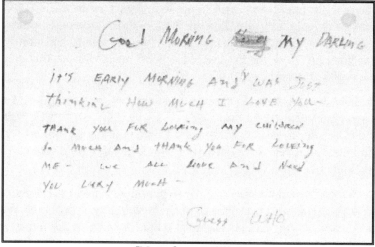

[Note from Willie]

We weren't in Fort Worth with Bobbie and Paul very long before we both decided that we were going to have to start making a living because money was running low for both of us. So it was back to the road we went, with Jimmy Day, a wonderful steel guitar player, joining us. We went to California for a recording session for Willie with Liberty Records. Willie tried booking himself for a while and I have to tell you we had lots of fun. But we sure didn't make much money and, worst of all, even though we were on a package show, we didn't draw any big crowds. I'm not sure if we noticed because we were in love, playing music and just doing what we wanted to do. We could meet our old buddies on the road, Little Jimmy Dickens, George Jones, and all the other great entertainers, and spend a whole day off in a motel room, playing music and having drinks, and eating. What a life!

But sooner or later you have to get back to the real world. One of the last big shows we were on while we were still in Fort Worth was one in Dallas with Red Foley, George Jones, Tammy Wynette and Bobbie Bare—well just a few of the biggies. In between shows Red came back to Fort Worth with us. This is the first time I'd seen him since the Jubilee in Springfield and, needless to say, we had to sober him up to go back for the last show. It was really sad to see such a great talent with an alcohol problem.

At this time, in between shows, George and Tammy flew to Mexico, Tammy got a divorce, and right away she married George. I guess I didn't realize anything was going on with them. I'd been too wrapped up in Willie and myself. Other things had happened too.

We were living now in Bobbie's house alone. She and Paul had gotten a larger house in Fort Worth. I remember when Willie took me to this wonderful furniture store in Fort Worth. He told me, "Buy anything you want and don't worry about the price." I furnished the whole house on the spot and how he made arrangements to pay for it I'll never know. At that time we didn't have any money for furniture.

Willie had started booking himself at different places around the country where he had been before: Houston, Phoenix, Tucson, Albuquerque, and finally we wound up in Las Vegas at the Golden Nugget with about a nine-piece band for two weeks. What an experience. I don't remember now where or who everybody was, but I do remember the date very well. Because on January 12, 1962, during the next to last show, I asked Willie if he'd like to marry me when we finished working that night.

My "flower girls" were Paul Buskirk from Houston, our guitar player Jimmy Day, and an up-and-coming fellow from Texas named Johnny Bush. Johnny and Jimmy both would follow us to Tennessee and John would later write Willie's opening song, Whiskey River. After our wedding, we all ate Mexican food, that's what we liked best, and I became Mrs. Willie Nelson. I guess I felt like we were already married, but now it was truly legal.

189

The kids visited with us while we were there, as I told you that Martha was also in Las Vegas. I'm not going to tell you that everything between Martha and me was fine, and it would take several years before it did get that way, but she was also going to marry again and have more children. So, considering everything, I don't guess we were doing too badly. Anyway, I was exceptionally happy and when I'm happy, I cook.

I cooked for all the band members. We had a kitchen in Vegas and I would skip the last show and go fry chicken or make beans and cornbread and, as the band told me later, everyone would be too full to do anything but go to bed. While we were out there, Pamper Music, or rather Hal Smith asked Willie if he'd go to Hollywood and open a branch office for them. So guess what? We were back on the road again and leaving our home in Fort Worth. We didn't stay in California too long, as Willie is just not an office person.

On November 20, 1963 we made the trip to Nashville to find a place to call home. It didn't take us long either. We rode up to Ridgetop, about 12-15 miles from Goodlettsville, and when we drove in the driveway to this house, I told Willie, "If that place has a fireplace in the kitchen, I don't want to see anything else." It did have one, and when the lady opened the door, she was making apple pies and we both fell for our new home right then and there.

Hal and Willie discussed everything later. I will never forget the day, our house and seventeen acres in Ridgetop, Tennessee. Now we needed to go back to California, arrange for all our furniture to come from Texas, and settle down on the "Ridge."

The next day we would be getting the news that President Kennedy had been killed and we flew back to California under black, black skies. When we circled Los Angeles to land that beautiful city of lights was so dark it was scary. Willie and I took the death of our president as personally as everyone else did and, for those days until President Kennedy would be buried, we were in mourning as was the rest of the world. But like everything else, everyone must go on and we felt that our life together was going to be so great. Now we had a home in Tennessee waiting for us and on New Year's Day, we would be in the home together.

We were going to leave California, work a couple of shows with Buck Owens in Washington state, drive to Las Vegas to see the kids for Christmas, and then go home to Tennessee. I have to tell you about one of the Washington dates we had. We were in Bellingham, Washington and Willie decided that we'd drive from there to Vegas, non-stop. By the time I'd been in the car, forever it seemed, I started fussing that I wanted out. He told me just a little farther then we'd stop and eat. I was feeling as if I was in a pumpkin and I didn't know what to do but go to sleep. At some point between Washington and Nevada, Willie woke me and told me he wanted me to listen to something he'd written for me. The song started with "Would be a comfort to know you never doubt me" and it ended with "because I love you in my own peculiar way." This was one of his most beautiful songs. All I said was "It's okay, I guess." Then I smiled and he smiled; it wouldn't have mattered if we'd had to drive forever.

We had a wonderful Christmas with the kids, lots of presents and food. Then it was on to Tennessee. We knew that bad weather had been forecast for Tennessee, but we didn't know just how bad until we got there, ice and snow.

The first thing we did was to try and get to our Ridgetop house, and the first thing we did when we got there was to get stuck. I thought I would be able to push and Willie thought he would be able to push. We were both miserably cold covered in snow, wet, and just about anything else you could name. When it seemed that our luck had just about run out, this old fella made it up to our car and, the way he still tells it today, said, "Children, what in the cat hair are you doing out in this?" He took us to his home, where it was nice and warm, and gave us hot food and introduced us to his wife, Ruby. They became our friends from that moment on, Mr. and Mrs. George "Tinker" Hughes. Later on, he came to work for us at the farm and remained with us until we left Tennessee some years later. What a man!

[My cornfield]

After the roads got to where we could get the car out, Willie and Mr. Hughes did just that. We went on out to the house and got both of our fireplaces going. We still didn't have our furniture yet, but lots of love went into the home that night. It wasn't long before the storm was over and everyone helped us to get ready for our furniture from Texas. Bobbie was helping on the Texas end, and Mr. Hughes, Hal Smith, and everyone at Pamper helped on our end. I'd never had a real home before, so I was busy as a bee trying to figure out all that had to be done. As I tell it now, we still lived out of our suitcases because I didn't know I had to unpack.

My Life with Willie

Those first months of being in Tennessee were wonderful. We had many plans for our home, which was finally turning into a reality. Mr. Hughes saw great possibilities for every kind of critter to live with us. We had chickens to begin with, and then Willie thought he should try to raise some hogs. Wrong!

By this time, Johnnie Bush had arrived in Ridgetop. He and Willie built this great corral out on the far end of the place. Then they went pig shopping and they came home with quite a few small pigs. As fast as they put one in the corral, it went out the other side. What a funny sight; all of us chasing little white pigs up and down the holler. The neighbors thought we were crazy. But we did catch them all.

We began to accumulate many things as the years rolled by. First, Mr. Hughes came to work for, and with, us. He just always seemed to be close around, and when his house burned in Ridgetop, it just seemed like the thing to do was to have him and Ruby work for us.

One morning after Mr. Hughes had done his chores, he left for a little while instead of visiting like he usually did. He came back to the house and said, "I need you to go look at something." I couldn't imagine what he wanted me to see. Anyway, I got in the truck with him and we drove off down the road. Past Mrs. Mullins's place, on around the curve, and he stopped at a gate a mile or so on down. He got out and opened the gate, got back in, and we drove through. A little farther up the road that was there, he stopped and what looked like maybe a house or basement had been. I asked him, what were we doing in there and whose property it was. And he told me, it was all for sale. Willie was always looking for more property and I thought Mr. Hughes had found it. I believe it had to be more than 200 acres because it seemed to run way on back. It was really beautiful and he said it was all for sale again. A couple of brothers owned it, I believe. I thought this could be great.

He drove to the back and then we got out to look around. You could see way down in the hollow and I thought how wonderful it would be for a cabin or a house. We walked a little farther and we saw two ponds, mostly dried up. But one had hoses in it going down to the valley. I asked Mr. Hughes, "What do you suppose those hoses are for?" And he told me, "People need the water." I couldn't figure it out for a minute, then I knew. I laughed and looked at him and said, "Moonshine, Tinker, moonshine." He laughed and said, "Right sister, right." So the farm became not only a place for the cattle Willie bought, but we had moonshiners too. What a deal!

Later on, Willie had Mr. Hughes and me pick out a herd of cattle from Porter Watts. These cows were nice. When the men brought them home, the first one out was a momma and she presented us with a new little calf. Porter said, "If that don't beat all! You people got an extra one for nothing."

The minute we bought the house in Ridgetop, Willie became "Country Willie." He wore bib overalls and a straw hat sometimes. So when he decided to go buy some pigs, he figured that would be a good idea. I don't know if he went to the sale in Springfield or where, but we ended up with a bunch of little pigs.

But first he had to build a place for them. I'm not sure, but I believe Johnny Bush, who worked in the band, decided he'd help. So they got the pen built up in the field from the house. And they backed the truck up to the pen and as fast as one went in, it went right out on the other side. Pigs running everywhere! We finally got them all back but you never could tell what he'd come home with.

We had dogs, and Queenee the farm dog and her pups, and poodles and Lord knows what else—chickens and ducks who loved the swimming pool. Then when we got the farm, we had horses and people who would just like a place to be.

[Mom, Willie, Grandma]

Country Willie was the best for Ridgetop. We had visitors, who became home folks. Willie would get a little guitar, and sit in the rocking chair, and sing, sing, old songs and new songs. And people didn't want to leave. It became home to a lot of folks. I'd cook and cook lots of good stuff to eat and in the winter the fireplace would look so friendly it was just impossible to leave us. Except for Mr. Hughes who would come in, take a nip, and say, "I'm going home and kick the clothes off Ruby and I'll see you in the morning." Then he'd laugh. We all loved him so much. He was just part of the family.

Lana, Susie and Billy were coming for summer vacation with us and, after the first year, we just didn't send them back home to Martha. I had, by this time, already asked to have Billy come live with us and Martha agreed. He arrived on an airplane in a little blue suit that I had sent him. He had a nametag on that said, "I belong to Shirley Nelson." I loved him so much. He didn't like it too well when the girls came out, but after a while they all go along just like kids do.

As Willie would tell you, the four years he had at Ridgetop with me and the kids were the best. I believe that too!

We were always doing lots of family things like holding hands at the table and saying grace, and sitting in the porch swing rocking and listing to the sounds of the night. Just a little later we had a swimming pool built, then Willie and I would sit on the steps and look at how big and fat the kids were growing. Some new additions came like ponies for them to ride.

Mr. Hughes told me that he was always saddling up or unsaddling something. All of them could ride really well. Willie built another corral out by the barn so he could practice roping, and I don't mind saying, he was a very good roper. Poor calves.

Willie was still going in to Pamper to see how his songs were going and he was still recording, but not like he wanted to. But at this point, it didn't disturb him so much. Then we were almost to his birthday and I decided to give him a party in our basement and invite just about everyone we knew. We cleaned and scrubbed everything. I made potato salad and fried chicken, and we had homemade Apricot wine. The two things Willie did were cut the wine down with vodka and paint the banister to the barn basement red. Well, needless to say, this was the most interesting part of the party. The paint didn't dry and he'd put the wine in a wine bag that you couldn't lay down, so someone always had to be carrying it, and drinking it, and everyone who attended the party had one red hand. It was so funny that the next day all you heard was, "So you went to the birthday party too!"

By this time a few of the musicians who loved Willie and me had moved to Ridgetop, so we had music at our party. In fact, we had weddings too. Johnny Bush decided to marry and I had to just about whip Willie Nelson. He wanted to be the preacher and I told him that he couldn't do it because he wasn't ordained. It took a lot of talk on my part, but he finally decided that maybe I was right. Wade and Grace Ray had moved back up on the curve from our house in a smaller house we'd bought. Wade was the greatest fiddle player of all time, and Grace is such a lovely person. There's a "Stand by your man" woman if ever there was one. We had some wonderful evenings with them. Willie and I would walk up the road and visit a while, maybe eat supper with them and then sit outside before walking home.

[Mom, Grandma, Grace Raye]

There weren't too many people who lived in Ridgetop when we moved there. It was just beautiful and it suited us just fine. By this time Mr. Hughes who we had met on that snowy night, helping us to get home, was working for us and Willie got him a new truck. He was so proud! Ruby, his wife, didn't come around much, but she was always close if I needed her.

Maggie, the black lady, was helping me get the house straightened up and she suggested her daughter, Pearlie Mae come and do laundry and ironing. And so I thought that was a great idea. Mr. Hughes or "Tinker" as he liked to be called, I never called him that, would go pick them up at home. They lived down in the valley. So it all worked out fine.

I found out from Mr. Young at his grocery store, the only one in town, on the corner before you turn back to our road home, Grandpa Jones lived on down the hill from Ridgetop. And his house was up on a steep hill from the little town. This lead to a funny episode, it had snowed some, one winter day, and Grandpa couldn't get to town. If it snowed in Ridgetop, you didn't go anywhere. He usually went to Goodlettsville to the grocery store. So he went to Mr. Young's grocery store to get his food. He came with his wheelbarrow. Then he started to walk back home and Mr. Young asked him if he needed any help. And Grandpa told him "No!" When he got to the bottom of his road and that steep hill, he stood there for a few minutes figuring out what to do. Then he started throwing his groceries up the hill. How he got up the hill, I don't know and he never would tell. What an idea! I think Ramona, his wife, probably threw him a rope.

Grandpa's best friend, fishing buddy, and hunting buddy, was String Bean, also from the Opry. He and his wife lived in a little house in the valley. And from our house a person could see String's but you couldn't see Grandpa's, too many trees, and brush, and rocks. String was quite a character himself. I had seen him at the Opry. He always wore overalls and carried a lot of money in the breast pocket of his overalls. I knew he was a genuine person, he and his wife but they didn't believe in banks. Later on, after I was gone from Ridgetop, both String and his wife were killed for money. String had come up on the porch and his wife; I believe she was getting out of the car when she was shot. They caught those old men but what a loss.

In Ridgetop, we had a post office, a grocery store and a doctor if there was anything else there I didn't see it. That's what we liked. There were several houses in the area where Mr. Hughes and Ruby lived. We had a small school run by the Seventh Day Adventist Church where the kids would go for a couple of years. Billy had to go to the first grade twice; he had a hard time learning to read. So we all tried to help him. There was a school at Greenbrier on up the road where they would go eventually. It was just a quiet little town.

I felt like I was in Paradise. I'd never known I could be this happy. Never having lived in a home, never having a family of my own, life was wonderful. I can't tell you that everything went along like heaven, but it sure was pretty close. My Little Guitar's life was now a home life, with Willie writing songs late at night, and me sometimes playing "Down in the Valley" for the kids. They loved all folk songs.

The first time I heard Willie sing "Red-Headed Stranger" was when we put the kids to bed and they asked him to sing it. Who would have thought he'd go on years later and make an album and a movie? We didn't have those thoughts back then.

Here's a little story about Wade and Grace and a present that they gave me. They had gone home to Illinois and brought me back a baby sheep. Now this sheep had to be fed and loved and, of course, had to have a name. We named her Pamper, after Pamper Music where Willie worked. She was one funny sheep. She slept in the house; in fact, Mr. Hughes was showing the house one time to some friends and he was saying, "This here's the bathroom, this is Billy's room, the living room, and the sheep's room." Isn't that funny? Well Pamper started growing and she eventually had to go outside, which she didn't like. She'd stand by the screen door of the living room and just cry. The kids were in there watching television and I was in the kitchen when, all of a sudden, I heard this crash.

Billy came running down the hall and said, "Shirley, Shirley, Pamper jumped through the screen and she didn't even say a word." I asked where she was now and he told me that she was in there watching television. It must have been her favorite program. We have so many stories about the animal life around our house in Ridgetop.

Probably the most famous one is the rooster, Shirley, and Ray Price. I had some of the most beautiful white hens anyone in the world would want to see, and Ray Price was, at that time, raising fighting cocks. He called and asked Willie if he could bring one out to our place because he was running out of room. Of course, Willie said yes and he put him in with my hens. Bad, bad, bad! For the next few days, every morning one of my beautiful hens would be dead. I had Willie call Ray and tell him that if he valued that rooster's life, he had better come and get him. He said he would, but he didn't and another hen bit the dust. Now it's "high noon" for that bird. Willie called Ray again and still nothing.

This time the rooster bit the dust and I gave him to our cleaning lady, Pearl, so she could have herself a chicken dinner. Her comment to me was, "Never in my life have we had a chicken that was so tough. I had an awful time getting the feathers off that thing." When Ray found out, he was furious. How dare we let anyone eat a $1,000 bird, and he vowed that he would never sing another of Willie's songs. Strong words then, but there's always another day, right?

Some years later, I did ask Willie who really shot the critter and he said, "I did," because he could see the hogs, turkeys, and everything else gone if I had shot through the barnyard. Maybe so.

Trouble in Paradise

One day, Willie had been into town with some friends and when he came home he was really quite drunk. He drove up in the driveway and got out of the car and came up our sidewalk onto the porch. I was waiting on the porch and we kind of had a little argument. He grabbed hold of the house column and just kind of hung on. I went in the house and he just stayed there on the porch. Over a period of time he had been studying judo or whatever that's called and he taught me a little bit. Just enough so I would be dangerous. I asked him to come in and he told me he'd just sleep on the porch all night. And I said, "No, you won't." By this time he was stumbling around and I grabbed hold of him and when I slung him around his head went through the top glass of the door. He was bleeding and I was crying and he just laid there, blood rolling down his face. And I was yelling, "Oh my God, I've killed America's greatest singer and songwriter!" Finally, I got him up, bandaged his head, cleaned the blood up and I saw he wasn't hurt real bad, but bad enough. He looked at me and said, "No more judo for you!" And all I said was, "I told you to come inside."

Another night I waited for him to get home and it seemed to get later and later. I always worried because our road was kind of winding there. Anyway, he finally came in and when I looked at him as he came in the house I saw he had had one too many with the boys or whoever. I was a little bit aggravated and he informed me if that's the way I felt, he'd go back to town. Anyway, I wasn't going to let him drive but he went on down to the car. He got in and sat there a little while. While he was doing that, I decided I needed to do something big. So he had a big thirty-eight revolver in the bedroom. I went out the door with it in my hand. Down the walk, I went only far enough that he could see I had his gun. I said, "You don't need to go to town," a couple of times. And he said he was going anyway. And the last time, he put his head out the car window. That's when I cocked that gun and pointed it straight at him. I believe he got sober, but I'm not sure. But he came out of that car on high. And he said, and these are his words, "If it's all the same to you I don't believe I'll go into town or anywhere else tonight." I believe he thought I'd just shoot the car. Maybe?

As I said, everything seemed to be going along nicely. The kids were going to school, doing homework, doing chores, and then Willie decided he needed to get back to work on the road. For a while, it was just with Wade and Jimmy Day in the car, but ambition called and he got his first bus. By this time, Willie's real mom and stepfather, his real father and stepmother, his sister, her husband, and their boys, musicians, girlfriends, and just friends began being at the farm. People would come to visit and never leave. But worst of all, Willie and I just didn't seem as close as we were. Hard to be close when you're miles apart, isn't it? If you recall, as I do, in the middle sixties there was lots of drugs; pills, uppers, downers, sleeping pills, and anything else was available.

I was upset about Willie being on the road and what was going on with him. We weren't having those talks we had always had. I guess we ceased to communicate. And nobody else would really talk to me. He would call me and tell me he was going to stay out on the road because he was tired. That was a lie, but I didn't know at the time he was with another woman. Eventually, Wade told me what was going on and I didn't believe him. I gave him an awful talking to. Wade quit Willie. Years later, I went to see Wade in Illinois and apologized. It broke my heart, as we had all been so close. I was so ashamed.

At that point in my life, I began to hide from everything. My heaven became hell. Lots of this time that I remember most, I really don't want to remember. I had no people of my own, except in Missouri, few friends of my own, because I was totally devoted to Willie and his friends. Maybe the biggest point of all of this is that I was getting close to thirty-nine and a real midlife crisis. Some of this is memories I'd like to forget, so maybe by writing them down, I will. I believe that we, Willie and I, were both at fault. But that's my opinion.

I love him as much today as I did then, but in a very different way. I feel sorry for him because he has missed the best parts of his life, with me, with Billy, not the roar of the crowd. He shut the door, like we didn't even exist. Maybe understanding has a great deal to do with it. When I found out, strictly by accident, that he had another family, a woman named Connie and new baby in Houston, I went completely nuts. The way I found out was she had the bill for the baby sent to the house in Ridgetop and I found it in the mailbox. When I confronted Willie, he lied and walked off from me. I did everything I could possibly do to destroy myself. My self-esteem was below bottom, my pride and my self-respect flew out the door. I believed that I was a complete failure at marriage and homemaking, and I did everything I could think of to get rid of me.

Naturally, Willie had already moved into town with the kids, making me believe that everything was my fault. But at this point, I didn't care. Then maybe, just maybe, God had decided to help me save myself. I got very ill with pneumonia, exhaustion, and confusion—you name it, I had it. At this point, thirty-nine years old, I called my family in Missouri and asked if I could come home. My dad said yes, so I hired someone to drive me to Chillicothe, Missouri in the middle of the night and I lay in the back seat of my car with six pairs of jeans, the same amount of sweatshirts, and the Little Martin.

When we drove up to my folks' house, Mom opened the door and she said I took one step and fell into her arms. Her words were, "Call the doctor now, we've got a very sick girl here, but she's home at last."

The Family
Music and lyrics by Shirley Nelson

It's so good to have the family back together
We have been apart for much to long
It's so good to have the family back together
All of us together here at home.
Each of us has grown up

And have families of our own
But we never can forget
Our happy days at home.

Mom and Dad grow older
Toward the twilight of their days
But all of us would travel far
To hear our momma say:

It's so good to have the family back together
We have been apart for much to long
It's so good to have the family back together
All of us together here at home.

So now I'm ill and the doctor came and gave me a shot and some medicine because I had pneumonia again. Mom and Grandma put me to bed and tried to get me to drink something, hot tea or something. I was just worn out. So sad, so upset, so unhappy. But nobody asked me what was going on, but I suspect they knew. Willie and I were not together anymore and I had come home. Every time that rolled around in my head I just got sicker, and my fever went up. Mom talked to Dr. Conrad and he thought maybe I should go to the hospital but Dad and Grandma said no. They said, leave me alone and I'd be okay. How they knew that I'll never know. But they knew me, at least Grandma did. But they were right.

In time I began to feel better, must have been the chicken soup. It was the better part of a month or more before I could even get up. I didn't want to get up. Chillicothe, Missouri again. I hadn't lived there since I was fifteen. There wouldn't be any more traveling with Willie. Actually, at the last I wasn't traveling with him anyway. I didn't have a job. I had money but I didn't want to use it all. I had my car, a few clothes, and a great pair of cowboy boots that Willie had bought me in Texas. They were going to send me my clothes from Tennessee later. So, when all hope was gone, and I wanted to forget, I drank. Mostly beer. But first, I had to have somebody to go with me. So I got my cousin, John Francis Scott. We'd always loved each other since we were kids. He was Dad's oldest sister, Aunt Ida's son. He would always say, "Aunt Idy's going to kill us." I had visions of her coming after both of us with a broom. We'd drink a whole bunch of beer and tell each other how much trouble we had with our lives. All I would do when he went home was go back to the folk's house and lay on the divan with my feet hanging off the arm and just lay there, like I was dead. And John would always see that I had gotten home okay.

That went on for two or three months. Either I was with John or just by myself roaming around, seeing what the town looked like, hopeless was the way I felt. No kids, no animals, no home, no husband who was off with another woman and a baby, nothing. Willie hadn't divorced me yet, and I hadn't divorced him. But in the meantime, he married Connie. I found that out later. It couldn't have been legal; he was still married to me. I didn't try to call him. I didn't try to find out where he was. I didn't really want to know anything about him at all. He had hurt me so bad, I just couldn't believe it.

After two or three months of me sleeping on the divan with my clothes on, which upset Grandma, a bright red pickup pulled in. Grandma's eyesight wasn't good by this time and she was easily upset especially by me and the way I was acting. Actually, nobody really spoke to me about the way I was acting. I guess they thought I was just going to lay on the divan and die, hanging over the edge. It was weird. It was terrible. A nightmare. And then one day a bright red pickup drove up. It was Mr. Haynes. Kenneth Haynes. I didn't recognize him but he told me who he was. He said, "I'm Fat Haynes." And mouthy me said, "Yeah I see you are." He said, "Get in; I'm going to take you to eat." And I thought "Why not?" He asked me what I was doing back in Chillicothe and I told him it wasn't any of his business.

I still couldn't place him but then he said, "I remember you when you were pickin' up nickels and dimes off of my tavern floor." I remembered Grandma used to take us on Saturday night to places that had music and my brother and I would dance and sing to the jukebox. And then people would throw money on the floor and we'd pick it up and put it in a sack and go home. Times were hard in the thirties, very hard. Then it dawned on me who he was. He was Mr. Haynes from Salle's Tavern. And he come to take me to eat. Needless to say, you don't bad mouth someone who could hit you with one hand and smash you or slap you into tomorrow. He was so big. I think he said something like, "You need to get yourself straightened up." And I think I said, "Shut up!" He didn't pay any attention to me. We had to go eat. I think from then on things began to change. He showed me it wasn't the end of the world. Where nobody talked to me, he talked to me all the time. He said, "I've always liked you since you were five years old. But you were always hard headed." He didn't ask me anything about Willie. Nothing about Tennessee. Nothing about trouble. I just guess he figured someday I'd start talking to him. I still had crying spells and hopelessness and feeling that I hadn't been a good wife, a good mother, a good housekeeper, or anything good. But I think I kind of began to come out of my shell. There would be life after Willie!

Has known what it is to
love and not be loved -
to want and not have -
to not understand and to be
misunderstood -
to be loved and not to be
able to return that love -
these things I have known.
But until now I have never
been loved, wanted, and understood
by someone that I love,
want and ~~understand~~ understand.
Until now I had never known
happiness -

I love you Shirley.
Your Willie

[Note from Willie]

[Me and Willie]

Afterword

I received a phone call on February 21, 1992 from my wonderful dear friend in Nashville, Joe Allison. I had been expecting this call and knew almost immediately what he was going to tell me.

Hiram Abiff Collie quietly passed away Wednesday evening, February 20th, in Nashville, Tennessee.

Biff had been fighting for several years, and successfully I might add, the battle with cancer. But this time, after being in the hospital and having several complications arise, he told Joe that he was ready to let this life go. This man had wonderful strength, great courage, and a strong love for our Savior, and I'm sure the gates were opened wide for him. He touched many lives while here on earth. As I have said repeatedly, he probably believed more in me and my abilities that any other living human being.

Joe had told him that I had called and my prayers were with him always. We had settled our differences many years ago and had continued to be friends. He was concerned that I was doing all right and that I was happy about my book. Even at the end, his concern for others showed through like a shining star. My grandma always told me, when I was small, that the brightest star I could see after Grandpa died was Grandpa. Now, when I look up, a new star will be shining brightly in the evening sky. "Hello Biff. You were very special to me!"

And now For Some Words From Two People
Who Are Very Dear to Me

Shirley & Willie and Others have been a work in progress. Obviously, living life in such a lifestyle developed the story as you have read it. Shirley has lived an incredible life... full of happiness, joy, sadness, and many other emotions. She is an amazing person, having grown up in a poor family, being self-taught and with an eagerness to succeed at such an early age. She developed into a beautiful young lady and continued to support herself and family. Following a dream of all she knew and having to continue to support her family she was transformed into a woman. The book unfolds into an amazing love story. The love story ended sadly, but Shirley continues to triumph. She survived the tragedies of losing the love of her life, besides giving up her god-given talent to be with him. She struggled to overcome these disasters in her life and after years of questioning why, she has found peace. As a niece to Shirley, I have always appreciated her. She not only has been gifted with the art of music, but as you have read, she is a very talented writer. I should have known because she has written many songs. She is simply just a natural talent. She is so many things to me... my confidant, my friend, my aunt, my second mom. I only wish for her that we could have seen her full potential. She gave her life to what she believed in and was cut short of her dreams. I believe in expressing herself through this book, she now has a much needed sense of closure. As we all know it is very difficult to let go of the things and the ones we love.

With Love,

Terri Minnick

211

Eddie's Note:

I met Shirley in 1991 when she came to me looking for a job. When she told me she had been married to Willie Nelson, I wondered why she would want a low-paying job working in a day treatment program for adults with mental retardation and developmental disabilities. She explained that after leaving Willie, she had, among many other things, worked with a similar population at the state hospital in Marshall, Missouri. As it was difficult to find people willing to work with our folks, let alone find someone with experience, I hired her immediately. It was one of the best decisions I have made in my life to date.

Over the years I have come to know and love Shirley. I have had the opportunity not only to read this book but have also been privileged to hear Shirley tell many of these and other stories firsthand. Additionally, over the years, Shirley has introduced me to many in the country music business including Willie, Johnny Cash, June Carter Cash, Anita and Helen Carter, Mel Tillis, Harold Bradley, Joe Allison, and many others. These experiences I will treasure for a lifetime as I will my time with Shirley. I believe that you will treasure getting to know and love Shirley as much as I have.

Eddie Melton

Appendix

Here is a list of the songs I wrote:

Catch The Breeze (1976) Shirley Nelson

Close Your Eyes (1962) Shirley Collie

The Cowboy (2005) Shirley Nelson

The Family (1996) Shirley Nelson

Forgive Him, Heart (1962) Shirley Collie

Hangin' On (1962) Shirley Collie

The Harlot (1969) Shirley Nelson

I Can't 'Cept It (1969) Shirley Nelson

I Feel That Old Feeling Coming On (1964) Shirley Nelson

I Have No Place to Go (1964) Shirley Nelson

I Hope So (1962) Shirley Collie

I'll Keep Hangin' On (1962) Shirley Collie

It Was Too Late (1962) Shirley Collie

I Wish It Was Me (2007) Shirley Nelson

Little Things (1968) Shirley and Willie Nelson

Lonely (2007) Shirley Nelson

My Faults Will Fade Away (1968) Shirley Nelson and Dave Kirby

Once More with Feeling (1970) Shirley Nelson (Recorded by Glenn Campbell)

Pages (1968) Shirley and Willie Nelson

Running Back to You (1968) Shirley Nelson

She's Still Gone (1968) Shirley and Willie Nelson

Take Me In Your Arms (2008) Shirley Nelson

The Shelter of Your Arms (1962) Shirley Collie

Thanks for Loving Me (1968) Shirley Nelson and Betty Spears

Til Death Do Us Part (1968) Shirley Nelson

Together (1996) Shirley Nelson

Union Baptist Church (1975) Shirley Nelson

The War (1999) Shirley Nelson

We Go Together (1969) Shirley Nelson and Dave Kirby

Where We Belong (1962) Shirley Collie

You're Not as Happy As You Thought You'd Be (1962) Shirley
 Collie

And I'm not through yet!

Lightning Source UK Ltd.
Milton Keynes UK
28 November 2009

146873UK00001B/28/P